The Works and Days of Svistonov

The Works and Days of Svistonov

by

Konstantin Vaginov

Translated and Annotated by
Howard Shernoff

CREATIVE ARTS BOOK COMPANY
Berkeley, California

For information contact:
Creative Arts Book Company
833 Bancroft Way
Berkeley, California 94710

ISBN 0-88739-341-1

Library of Congress Catalog Number 00-103040

Printed in the United States of America

Table of Contents

The Short Life, Changing Times of Konstantin Vaginov

Konstantin Konstantinovich Vaginov (real name Vagenheim) was born in St. Petersburg on 4 April 1899.[1] His father, gendarme officer Konstantin Adolfovich Vagenheim, came from a long since Russified German family that had settled in St. Petersburg in the eighteenth century. His mother, Lyubov Alekseyevna, was the daughter of a wealthy Siberian landowner and owned several buildings in St. Petersburg.

Konstantin received one of the best educations to be had during his day, studying at the Y. Guryevich Gymnasium from 1908 to 1917. After graduation he entered the law department of Petrograd University. Soon thereafter, though, he was mobilized by the Red Army, which was in the midst of losing badly to the Germans. He fought at the Polish front during the war and then beyond the Urals during the civil war that resulted from the subsequent Bolshevik coup d'état.[2] In 1921 Vaginov returned to Petrograd but was not reinstated at the university because of his distinctly non-proletarian background. He changed emphasis and graduated from the Institute of Art History. Vaginov remained in the city of his birth, Petersburg turned Petrograd turned Leningrad, practically without interruption until his premature death a little more than one decade later.

As did so many budding young Pushkins, Vaginov began writing verse while still at gymnasium, using Beaudelaire as a model and the prism of Symbolist poetry as a viewfinder on the world around him. Although he eventually found his own voice and shirked most dominant literary influences, one obsession was never to leave him: a fascination with antiquity. Even as a child he collected and studied literature on ancient archeology and history. His childhood favorite was a multi-volume piece of research by 19th century British historian E. Gibbon entitled *The History of the Fall and Ruin of the Roman Empire*. A particularly strong influence on the young writer was made by the work of British art scholar and writer Walter Pater, described by P. Muratov as a man who "simply lived in the past, as it was for him actually more real than the present."

Reading Vaginov's prose as well as poetry, one senses that the young author indeed yearned for a life free from the unseemly encroachments of the present. In addition to wearing antique rings on his long, thin fingers and having a surprising knowledge of old dances and exotic culinary recipes, Vaginov refused to acknowledge electric lighting. By 1930 he still had not installed electricity in his apartment, preferring, like his character Andrey Svistonov, the light of candles burning in antique candlesticks.

In the early twenties, in spite of the hardships of the War

Communism era, Petrograd was alive with literary and artistic activity. It was a city of circles, workshops, readings, and makeshift salons. The House of Arts had been opened, hosting enthusiastic scribes from all generations. It also housed a functioning literary workshop led first by N. Gumilyov and later, after Gumilyov's tragic end, by K. Chukovskiy. Vaginov attended the workshop, where as he put it, "thronged those for whom creativity took the place of bread and warmth." Poetess Ida Nappelbaum recalls that Vaginov "was the smallest, thinnest, most weak-voiced, and most frail, but immediately became significant and important. He sat at a distance from Gumilyov at the end of the long table, and when he stood and commenced reading, a new world appeared, thrilling and comparable with nothing and no one. He read softly and with his loose enunciation. But everyone listened and allowed himself to be carried off to that illusory world dreamed up by the poet."

In summer of 1921 the poet, along with N. Tikhonov and S. Kolbasev, entered the so-called Islanders Group. In distinction to many other literary groups, the Islanders did not emerge with a sweeping manifesto; they strove for the union of a varied creative individuality.

The Islanders convened at different locations, including the House of Arts (where Kolbasev lived), the Poets' Union on Liteynyy Prospect, Tikhonov's flat, and the residence of poetess Vera Lure, who two years later recalled how in her apartment on the Moyka Canal, towards eleven in the evening, the poets arrived and "sat until two thirty in the morning (there was a three o'clock curfew in the city), heating the little stove with dried wood, smoking foul cigarettes, drinking endless cups of tea. . . reading works. If verse was being read, then Vaginov was requested to be last: he had such an enormous stock of work that we were afraid that after him there would be no time for anybody else. Kostya [Konstantin], petite and homey, seated himself usually on the floor near somebody's leg."

Following the summer, the Islanders came out with their debut collection, printed by typewriter in an edition of about twenty copies, in which Vaginov for the first time published his poetry. In spring of 1922 they managed to publish a typeset collection, also featuring Vaginov's verses. In it was an announcement for a soon-to-be published book of Vaginov's verse entitled *Petersburg Nights* and a book of his prose entitled *Monastery of our Father Appollon*. Lack of funds, a frequent occurrence in those years, kept the publications from being realized. Nonetheless, Vaginov's poetry, appearing from time to time in other Petrograd anthologies as well, did not pass unnoticed, receiving favorable mention from several notable critics.

By 1922 Vaginov, by his own account, "belonged to practically every association of poets in the city." He had joined the Fofanov Ring of Poets, under whose copyright his first book of poems, *Journey into Chaos*, was released. He belonged to a group of emotionalists led by Mikhail Kuzmin, and he visited a union of young poets called the Sounding Shell. He even attended gatherings of proletarian poets held in various houses around the city. The young composer of verse fed himself on the city's atmosphere of literary life. Kind and tolerant, he was loved and accepted by all. In company he did not try to stand out, preferring to listen to others, whom he won over with his fine manners and delicacy. He spoke little but was always willing to read his work. And of course in his verses he invoked the times, countries, and events of the distant past, often substituting logical development of images with whimsical association, in the manner of Mandelshtam. He brought a phantasmagoric antiquity to an increasingly materialistic contemporary world.

Although by the end of 1922 Vaginov had decided that the period of working as part of a circle was over for him—"I have gone through every poetic circle and organization; it long ago has ceased to be necessary for me... I want to work alone"—his concern for the ruin of culture brought on by Bolshevism was shared by many writers, artists, and intellectuals of his day.

In the brutality of the day, concern for the preservation of culture was accompanied by concern for the preservation of the would-be custodians of that culture. "That they would take you, throw you in prison, and put you to great expense seemed senseless at the time; that they would interrogate, torture, and hold your mouth either to bring on death or your exit from the literary world (as they did with Zamyatin and Kuzmin) began to come to light in more and more distinct forms...." wrote N. Berberova.

Vaginov attempted to save from destruction any intact objects of the culture of the past. In all of Vaginov's novels, rarities from the book world are indexed: the library of writer Svistonov is full of rare publications on everything from culinary arts to cosmetics. Books, in fact, serve as a major character in the novel.

Vaginov himself, who wrote, "I was reared on the arts

from the cradle," was a passionate bibliophile. One might meet him among the Petrograd secondhand booksellers located along Liteynyy Prospect, and he often visited the Aleksandrovskiy Flea Market, where books from confiscated libraries were taken and sold by weight. On one occasion, a portion of the library of Aleksandr III arrived, and Vaginov was overjoyed to acquire a segment of the unique publications. When Vaginov had any money whatsoever, he purchased books on Old French and Italian languages, translations of Latin authors, sketchbook journals, letters, anything that had the smell of a bygone era. On his own, Vaginov studied Old French and Italian so as to read forgotten authors, began studying Spanish in pursuit of his dream to translate the Spanish Baroque poet Góngora, and even tried his hand at translating Greek prose.

Vaginov collected not only books. In that same flea market, he acquired for next to nothing ancient objets d'art which he displayed in the two small rooms of his apartment on Canal Griboyedova. He also collected apparently useless objects such as cigarette boxes and candy wrappers. Collecting, naturally, runs as a theme through all of Vaginov's novels. One of the more far-reaching treatments of the topic is found in *Works and Days*: the main character, Svistonov, collects not only press clippings but the very people necessary for his novel.

The spectacle created by Vaginov's deliberate infusing a dogmatic present with objects and attitudes of an obliterated past often has been described as carnival-like. This peculiarity of Vaginov's prose was esteemed highly by Mikhail Bakhtin, an investigator of "carnival culture," who was struck as well by the cast of eccentrics constantly parading before the reader of Vaginov's prose: "Here is a veritable carnival writer," wrote the great philosopher and literary critic.

The relationship between author and character, a recurring theme for Vaginov, does not escape infection by this blinking world of grotesque carousel figurines. In *The Goat Song,* Vaginov's first novel, the character of the Author asks: "Will emptiness manifest around me if I actually banish [my characters]?" In *Works and Days,* his second novel, the distressing answer is given: after having "transferred" all of his acquaintances into his novel, the writer/collector Svistonov feels "everything around him thinning with each day" until he himself is "completely locked inside his novel."

Just as Svistonov shows his characters, all of whom hope to be rendered as significant individuals in his novel, no mercy, Vaginov shows Svistonov no mercy, demonstrating how art unimpassioned with a love for life and people is bound to doom its creator. Ultimately it was Vaginov who emerged as the only player in this game to be shown mercy—by a fate that sent him a fatal case of tuberculosis in 1934. Were it not for that illness, he surely would have perished during the Stalinist purges of Leningrad that claimed the lives of so many talented artists and writers. In fact, shortly after Vaginov's death, his mother was arrested on an order to arrest her son as well. But the order was too late. Konstantin Konstantinovich, like his fictional hero and that hero's heroes, had been transferred finally into another world.

TRANSLATOR'S FOREWORD

> In point of fact, any translation that does not sound like a translation is bound to be inexact upon inspection.
>
> – Nabokov

The most unfortunate thing about a translation, especially one from a non-Germanic or non-Romantic language, is that its quality is judged most of the time by those who cannot read the original text.

Although the translator himself may benefit from this arrangement, the reader usually winds up the loser. As long as the translator is not held accountable for his task by a knowledgeable third party—as long as he is left to his own devices, as it were—he is left with only one sure-fire method for garnering praise and ensuring success for his work: to make his version of the original as dazzling as possible.

But we know that not every writer dazzles with his prose. Not every writer is eloquent, fluid, and crisp at every turn. Some genres practically require repudiation of artful prose, and some authors have changed literature forever by spurning the elegantly turned phrase.

In his prime as a writer, Konstantin Vaginov was an erudite young man, an innovative poet, and a skillful novelist. One ought to be on safe ground translating his creations; the model ought to be sound enough. But let us remember that the time frame here is the 1920s and the place is Soviet Russia, or rather, Imperial Russia freshly overthrown by a very small number of uneducated young thugs calling themselves Bolsheviks.

Intellectualism and spiritualism, valued during Vaginov's formative years, were not only no longer esteemed, but condemned. Primitive materialism was the rule of the day, injecting daily life with boorish vulgarity and the creative arts with defiant philistinism. Glaring brilliance in prose writing seemed gratuitous to both author and, more perilously, to the powerful ideologue masquerading as literary critic.

Vaginov's answer to these conditions was a style of prose that, although not parodic in the strictest sense, reflects the unrefined existence into which his city and his world had fallen. Occasionally even with bitterness it serves up the rawness, roughness, and disregard for tradition that characterized the new, Soviet culture. More often, however, it delivers scenes that border on the grotesque—some might even say the Kafkaesque—with such restraint that the translator must be very careful to render their nuances.

Indeed the very first lines of *The Works and Days of Svistonov* are a translator's nightmare: a deliberately inelegant description of a woman bathing in a kitchen. And if faithfully done, the translation is doomed before the reader reaches the novel's second paragraph, for one cannot imagine an opening passage whose form is more lacking in grace and whose content is more devoid of dignity. There must be a problem here, thinks the reader, and that problem must be the translation. Without knowing Russian, he or she simply can feel it.

It would not be difficult to turn Vaginov's prose into slick and innocent lyricism at every turn, and if the early century British translators who first brought us Dostoyevskiy and Tolstoy had gotten their hands on Vaginov's work, that is precisely what they would have done. But slick and innocent Vaginov is not; and lyric—only in the service of calculated juxtaposition.

In the same way that the literator Svistonov, in his search for characters to put into his novel, only occasionally stumbles across a figure worth lingering over for more than a standard measure of time, the reader of Vaginov's novel only sporadically runs into an expressive gem amidst what can be, at times, apparently featureless prose. Naturally, it is at these times that the author, at least unconsciously a product of Russian Symbolism, reveals more about his "plot" than at others. However, even here one must be mindful that Vaginov composed his novels during a time of great dilettantism as well and took the liberty of serving up that element of literary society with characteristic irony.

There will be readers on whom Vaginov's brand of prose will be lost. Realism, so cherished in America, has never been a strict prerequisite for European or Russian novels and is largely missing from Vaginov's oeuvre. Furthermore, like many Russian writers of his era, Vaginov at times can be too smart for his own good, relying on arcane references, subtle intratextual allusions, and careful diction often cleverly disguised. His cinematic approach to rendering setting, moreover, may be slightly less eye-opening today than it was in the twenties, when motion pictures were just becoming an exciting new part of popular culture.

Yet the translator's task is to refrain from shepherding any lost readers back into the flock, however tempting it may be, with embellished phrases and beautified words of his own invention. It is not his job to smooth the road or even to make it fit for modern conveyance. It is his duty and privilege, some say his art, to be as attentive as possible to the original text and as sensitive as possible to the language into which he forces that oddly foreign text. No more, no less. Only then does a quality translation result, and only then do all readers emerge winners.

I wish to thank Olga Slavina, who introduced me to the works of Konstantin Vaginov, convinced me to translate them, and tutored me on their finer points. I also thank my good friend Sergey "Pit" Selivanov, who carefully reviewed my translation and sparred with me for hours over details large and small. I dedicate this first ever English-language edition of *The Works and Days of Svistonov* to my late Grandmother Arlene, whose family fled Russia many years ago and who always wondered what on earth I was doing there. Grandma, now you know.

A NOTE ON RUSSIAN NAMES

Readers of Russian fiction occasionally can be confused by traditional Russian forms of personal address. In formal or official situations, Russians address each other by using both a person's first name and his or her patronymic. The patronymic invariably is derived from the first name of the person's father. For example, Sergey Ivanovich is literally "Sergey, son of Ivan," and Tatyana Andreyevna, "Tatyana, daughter of Andrey."

Additionally, Russians are extremely fond of using diminutives when addressing each other in familiar situations. Although some diminutives may be slightly derogatory (in this novel there are no diminutives expressing contempt), the majority are used to express closeness and/or tenderness.

Listed below are some of the more frequently encountered formal names and diminutives in this book. Note also that all Russian words carry stress on only one syllable; the stressed syllable of each name is indicated below.

Character	Formal Name	Diminutives
Andréy Svistónov	Andrey Nikoláyevich	Andryúsha, Andryúshenka
Svistonov's wife		Lénochka
Kukú	Iván Ivánovich	
Kuku's girlfriend	Nadézhda Nikoláyevna	Nádenka
The old couple	Tatyána Nikándrovna Pyotr Petróvich	Tánya Pétya
Psikhachyóv	Vladímir Yevgényevich	

Experienced readers will notice that the spelling of many Russian names in this book differs from that which they may have met in other translations. The reason is that I have employed a direct system of transliteration according to which a Russian name containing seven Cyrillic characters (not including silent characters), is spelled in English with seven corresponding Latin characters (excepting names containing a Cyrillic character without a Latin correspondent; these characters take two Latin ones). This system nowadays is more popular among practical linguists who wish to achieve a more honest rendering of Russian names in the Latin alphabet and to ensure that Russian names written in English are distinguishable, for example, from Polish ones.

The Works and Days of Svistonov

CHAPTER ONE
STILLNESS

Having removed her dress and taken a Turkish towel, his wife, as always in the evenings, bathed in the kitchen. Splashing herself with water, she pressed one nostril and blew with the other. Cupping her hands beneath the faucet and lowering her head, she rubbed her face with wet palms, stuck her fingers into pallid ears, washed her neck and the top of her back, then ran one arm along the other up to the shoulder.

Seen through the window was a little house they called "the cottage," recently painted a white hue, with illuminated square windows and surrounded by snow-covered trees; two walls of the St. Petersburg Conservatory; part of the cement Academic Theater building with its long windows shining brightly by evening. Behind all this, a little to the right—a bridge and a thoroughfare where the Milk Union stood, a pharmacy loomed, and the Pryazhka Canal muddied as it flowed into the Griboyedova Canal not far from the sea. [1] Giving onto the Pryazhka was a large building with a garden.[2]

Svistonov was looking out the window at the area where the theater, the pharmacy, and the Milk Union all met.

The canal passed behind the building in which Svistonov lived. In spring, mud scoops appeared on the canal; in summer, small boats; autumn, drowned young women.

Behind the canal ran streets with taverns, with deranged faces and wheezing throats of drunken women peering out from behind corners.

Svistonov yearned to once again don a blue-banded student's cap and galoshes and head out into the nighttime city with its Admiralty and spire, General Staff Headquarters and archway, St. Catherine's Church, City Duma, Public Library. He yearned for youth.

Behind the window everything had long ago vanished. In the apartment it was quiet. Only the clock, which had survived various relocations yet had been deprived of its chime, ticked in the dining room.

Svistonov had a dream.

A man is hurrying along a street. The man, Svistonov recognizes, is himself. Walls of buildings are translucent, several not so, others—in ruins. Behind transparent walls are quiet people, still drinking tea at their table covered with oil-cloth. The head of the family, a craftsman, having pulled a chair away from the table, plucks a guitar while studying the elongated reflection of his face in the samovar. The children, kneeling in the chair and holding up their heads with their little fists, gaze away the hours, here at the lamp, here at the stove, here at a corner in the floor. It's rest after the workday.

Behind another transparent wall sits a clerk. He smokes a pipe, affects an American expression, and for hours watches the smoke twisting, a drowsy fly on the windowsill crawling, or in a window across the courtyard, a man sitting and scouring the newspaper for news of some entertaining murder or another.

And there, across the street, all the widows have gathered and are gabbing about the intimate details of their interrupted married lives.

Svistonov sees that he, Svistonov, come daytime will pursue everyone as if they were unusual wild game. Here he will close in on a basement apartment as a hunter would a wolf hole and peer in to see if a person is there; here he will sit for a while in a garden and visit with a citizen reading a newspaper; here he will stop a small child on the street, give him candy, and commence making inquiries about his parents; here he will discreetly drop by a small grocery shop, browse around, and discuss politics with the clerk for a while; here, playing at being a compassionate individual, he will give ten kopecks to a beggar and take great pleasure in his little charade; here, passing himself off as a handwriting analyst, he will make rounds of all the well-known personages in the city.

In the morning, having looked at his watch, Svistonov forgot everything. Trying not to wake his wife, he sat down, partially dressed, to his editing. He corrected a thing or two, altered a thing or two, then hurried off to the Writers' Club.

Everyone was already sitting around, in hats and beanies, exchanging bits of gossip and the latest news. The editor, a rouged and heavy-set woman, was smoking and reading a manuscript behind her worn desk. From time to time she glanced off to the side and sighed. She found the conversations interesting, even occasionally enjoyable, but the racket of footsteps and the peals of laughter distracted her. Svistonov greeted the editor and the others. The editor offered him her hand and fell back to her reading.

The writers sat around talking for about four hours, waiting, seeing who would be the first to rise. Having sat his share, like everyone, and taken pleasure in the conversations, like everyone, Svistonov disappeared into the elevator and found himself on the Prospect of the 25th of October.[3] It was already rather late, and writers and journalists were scampering from the publishing house to the printing house and back again. Warmed by the springtime sun, they were discussing how Kruglov writes like Chesterton, how nice it would be to go to the Crimea, how nice it would be to bring off the kind of book that could be released every year. They were going down to the Moscow Shareholders Society, eating fried piroshki, reading the evening edition of the *Red Gazette* to see if there was anything about themselves in the news, buying the Moscow magazines and checking there as well to see if they had been written about. When they found something, they laughed. The rubbish they write! Occasionally a student-journalist approached and asked what they were working on. Then the writers lied.

It wasn't an easy job to sit in the editorial office for four, sometimes even five, hours. By five o'clock the writers' heads pounded. Fatigued, they arrived home, had dinner, and lay down to catch an hour-long nap. Come evening, satisfied that the day had passed and that now they would be unable to work, they went with their wives to visit an acquaintance for a cup of tea.

Svistonov in the evening lay in bed and thought. What to read up on? The antique church plate that might serve useful for his new short story? Or perhaps take a few lessons from Mérimée on conciseness and precision. Or perhaps grab a volume from the *Collection de l'histoire par le Bibelot,* as trifles can be surprisingly informative and can help catch an epoch unawares.

But Svistonov was too lazy to put on the slippers he had stitched together out of castor during times of great shortages and hunger. He did not leave his blanket, did not get up on the stool, did not quickly retrieve any books. Instead he turned to his wife and started talking about things overheard at the office.

"Lenochka," he said, lighting a cigarette.

Lenochka put down Panayeva's *Memoirs* and, reclining on her elbows, looked at her husband.

"Count Ekespar," Svistonov said, inhaling languidly, "called his gypsy lover 'Dulcinae.' He divided his holdings into satrapies and placed at the head of each satrapy a satrap. He gave out rations to his men like Genghis Khan—three sheep a month for soldiers, two for officers."

"Is that so?" asked Lenochka.

"He dreamed of forming a pan-Mongolian empire with the German official language and moving the Golden Horde west."

"There's a topic for you. You could make an interesting tale out of it."

"I still haven't told you," Svistonov livened up, "that he proclaimed himself the Buddha, kept up a correspondence with Chinese generals, and even found a pretender to the imperial throne—some kind of Anglicized Chinese prince who lived in America and blushed whenever he was even called Chinese!"

Stretching out beneath the blanket, Svistonov went on smoking. He gazed at the ceiling, then turned and gazed at the wall.

"Oh, Lenochka," he said, "what a pity I've never been to Mongolia. Monasteries are the very breath of that country. German accounts give it no breath whatsoever. I could maybe join up with Kozlov's expedition … take a vacation from the evening *Red* …." No sooner had he closed his eyes and begun to nod off when somewhere off to the side a thought came to him about hunting and hunters.

He felt like writing. He grabbed a book and began reading. Svistonov did not create systematically, a world did not suddenly take shape in front of him, everything did not suddenly become clear, and he did not write then.[4] On the contrary, his creations emerged from vague notations in the margins of books, from stolen similes, from adroitly rewritten pages, from overheard conversations, from recast gossip.

Svistonov lay in bed and read—that is, he wrote, as for him it was one and the same thing. With a red pencil he outlined a paragraph; with a black one he entered it into his manuscript in a reworked state, not worrying about overall meaning and cohesion. Meaning and cohesion would come later.

Svistonov read:

In a viniferous valley of the Alazan River, amidst a great number of enveloping gardens, stands the city of Telav, once the capital of the Cahetian Tsardom.

Svistonov wrote:

Chavchavadze sat in a Cahetian wine cellar and sang songs of the viniferous valley of the Alazan River, of the city of Telav, once the capital of the Cahetian Tsardom. Chavchavadze was quite intelligent and loved his motherland. His grandfather had been a cavalry captain in the Russian services—but no, no, he had to return to his people. With loathing Chavchavadze looked at the merchant sitting nearby singing a song by Shamil and playing the guitar. "Huckster," mumbled Chavchavadze. "Low-life, lackey." The merchant looked at him plaintively. "Don't begrudge me, I'm a good man."

Having written this fragment, Svistonov put the page aside. "Chavchavadze," he repeated, "Prince Chavchavadze. And what on earth does engineer Chavchavadze think of Moscow?[5] All right," he decided, and continued reading about the death of Tsar Irakliy and the sorrow of his wife, Darya.

On low divans the dignitaries' wives sat wrapped from head to toe in long white shawls and, beating themselves on the chest, loudly bewailed the loss of the tsar. Opposite the women, to the right of the throne, government officials, without speaking and with mournful faces, took their places according to rank. Above everyone sat the highest ministers, and behind them, the masters of ceremonies with broken staffs. From the window could be seen the tsar's favorite steed, standing by the palace gates, saddled upside down. Beside the horse a bare-headed official sat on the ground.

"Great," thought Svistonov. "Chavchavadze is a Georgian ambassador under Paul I, and Count Ekespar, a descendant of Teutonic knights. Well, perhaps not Teutonic ... I better check ...."

Distant prospects for future work began to come into view, images appeared. "A Pole," he thought. "There would need to be a Pole. And also a bastard son, one of Bonaparte's, commanding a Russian regiment in the eighties."

Amorous eyes of Poland, their gaze fastened upon France. Henry III has escaped, Bonaparte is on St. Helen's Island. Napoleon III, resurrection unsuccessful. "Now France and Poland are again two culturally benighted sisters," thought Psheshmitski, walking past the Cathedral of Notre Dame, "and a third knight looks upon us—Georgia."

Svistonov sat down on the bed. "Indeed, let's use Paris," he thought, looking at the floor. "I need to go to the bookshops tomorrow." Having wrapped himself in the blanket, Svistonov began to snore.

In the morning, after a visit to the editorial office, he headed off with his briefcase to Volodarskiy Prospect and commenced making rounds of the bookshops like a woman with a reticule in Gostinyy Dvor.[6, 7]

The owners and the clerks inquired about his new novel, commented that it should be interesting to read, that here is a curious little book, perhaps he might recommend this little book to one of his acquaintances.

The free and easy days of books had come to an end, and rare books once again had become rare. The booksellers' business in general went poorly. Libraries no longer sold them 15 kilos of books for only a ruble and 20 kopecks.

Svistonov rummaged around looking for Polish emigrant books, looking for books on Georgia, on the Baltic region. The booksellers, withdrawing to a corner, drank vodka, conversed with the steady customers, watched the street from afar.

A contented Svistonov headed home. He had found the following:

1) *Recveil de diverses pieces, servans à l'histoire de Henry III roy de France et de Pologne.* A Cologne, chez Pierre du Marteau MDCLXII

On this book an ex libris with the coat of arms of D. A. Benkendorf had been crossed out; on the coat of arms was the motto *Avec Honneur.*

2) *Russian Pomerania,* ed. 1, published by Y. Samarin. Prague 1868

3) *Essai critique sur l'Histoire de la Livonie . . .* par C.C.D.B. MDCCXVII

. . .and still many others in supple pigskin and calfskin bindings.

Svistonov did not like electricity, thus candles were already burning in his apartment.[8] Lenochka was sitting at the table reading.

. . . I lay in a luxurious bed and slept very peacefully for about four hours, and waking up, I saw lying on the window a flute which I took and began playing an aria on in honor of the beautiful girl in the portrait, unaware that this flute had been made with wonderful craftiness, for as soon as I began playing, at that very instant all of the fountains let out their water with great noise, and the different kinds of birds in the garden, each by his own nature, began singing loud songs which caused a number of trees to cast off their fruit. I became frightened because of that strangeness and immediately ceased playing, afraid that someone would come and kill me dead for my audacity. Since in the meantime the day was giving way to evening, I had not even considered where else to leave this lovely place for, but remained in this gazebo to spend the night, and on the next day spent the first part of the day here. But seeing as there was not a person in the garden... [9]

Svistonov had bought this worn and despised book amidst miscellaneous bric-a-brac at the Palm Sunday Bazaar several years back when he had been interested in literary styles.

Lenochka sat by the candles. The novel bored her. At any rate, it was far less interesting than Walter Pater. She had grown hungry but was waiting for Svistonov so that they could have dinner together. She went over to the middle window and looked to see if Svistonov was coming.

She returned to finish her reading, then remembered she had yet to dust today. She went into the next room, set the brown ladder in place, and took to wiping Svistonov's books. "How long it's been since Andryusha wrote verse," she thought, moving the ladder. She took down Svistonov's notebooks and stood still with her dust rag on the ladder.

She leafed through Svistonov's notebooks of verses, once considered unintelligible and then having become too intelligible, and came across a lock of her hair and dried flowers. The verses had faded, had paled with time, but for her they shined all the same.

Lenochka ran the dust rag along the spines of the books. There were so many books here now, but my God, the kinds of books! Diary manuscripts of unknown functionaries; little books used every day by lustful students; a correspondence of a wife with her husband, apparently a railroad employee; thin little brochures printed by prolific hacks; philosophical books perfunctorily written by actors; oversize books in leather bindings; scrapbooks of teenagers; a Saint Petersburg calendar from Christmas to the summer of 1754 with the following entries: 6th, Let blood from my foot, 19th, Snowed, 28th, Bought straw. Cosmetology books from *Gli ornamenti della donna,* (Giovanni Marinello, 1562) to most recent; cookbooks; home remedy books; books devoted to dances and card games no longer in existence; shelves with classics; and tomes and packages of books lying or standing every which way.

Taking a seat on the ladder, Lenochka began reading the verses. She read and recalled where and when Andryusha had written them, how he had been dressed, how she had been dressed. But the doorbell chimed, and Lenochka, having moved the ladder aside and dropped her dust rag, answered the door.

Svistonov read the newspaper and with a red pencil circled phrases that Lenochka was to cut out and paste on sheets of paper.

The soup was getting cold.

"Why don't you read later," Lenochka said. "Tell me something."

"What's there to tell you?" Svistonov replied and continued reading.

"Tell me at least what the weather's like today," Lenochka said, trying to strike up a conversation. "Have the buds blossomed? And where will we go for summer?"

"To Toksovo most likely," lazily mumbled Svistonov, standing up. "Wonderful air there."

He went to lie down. He had drunk a little wine with dinner and therefore wasn't able to read and write. Lying on the divan, he watched Lenochka and followed how she walked around the room burrowing among the books.

"Lenochka, read some clippings," he said.

Lenochka got her sheets of paper covered with press

clippings and, sitting down close to the candles, began reading.

***

November, 1914

According to wounded Germans, the mood of the soldiers is highly dispirited. Officers are constantly telling them about victories, but the soldiers no longer believe these stories.

***

21 June 1913

"Ottoman"
A model and perfection!
To smoke her a delectation,
How our cigarette *extra fin* –
Will give you pleasure en plein!!!
Glory to Shaposhnikov's wares and store,
Criez, messieurs, bravo, encore!!!
– Uncle Mikhey

***

29 July 1913

AMERICAN MILLIONAIRES' BALL
... the majority of the women arrived at the ball in either simple country dresses or in costumes of popular fairy tale hero-

ines. With this, they wished to emphasize their critical attitude towards militant suffragettes.

***

FLEA INVASION

The number of fleas in the city has multiplied drastically. Apartment buildings, hotels, theaters, and cinemas all complain of the appearance of masses of fleas. Poor cleaning of premises fosters the rapid spreading of fleas during summer. The Sanitation Department has been addressed by entire buildings with the request to rid apartments of fleas. The cleaning will be performed using a gas and will cost very little.

***

Several hotels have issued a request to be saved from bedbugs. This work also is being carried out with great dispatch.

***

HEATED SPEECHES AGAINST GERMAN DOMINATION . . .

***

"Lenochka, how many times have I asked you to take all the clippings and repaste them in chronological order. I don't think it can be that difficult! And what's more, how many times have I asked you to place the date and the name of the newspaper on all the clippings, even on the most insignificant ones. It would really make the work easier you know!"

Lenochka sorted through the clippings, gazed at her hero.

"All right, all right," she calmed him. "I'll get it done, don't worry."

"And the month, and the date, and the name," Svistonov repeated.

But in general he had been pleased with the reading. It had stirred his imagination.

Lenochka grabbed her darning egg and began to darn a pair of socks. The candles in alabaster candlesticks the shape of grape leaves crackled. Svistonov grew bored.

"Lenochka," he said, "read some novellas."

He called other newspaper clippings "novellas."

Lenochka stood up from the easy chair, retrieved a small volume in Moroccan leather, and began leafing through it.

"The tailor," requested Svistonov.

That was novella thirty-three.

Novella Thirty-three

The Novelist-Experimentalist

Before writing something, one must himself live through the phenomenon to be depicted.

This principle is professed by tailor Dmitriy Schelin. For about two years now he has been writing a kind of "novel from contemporary life," with all of that life's horrors.

Two months ago Schelin needed to conclude a chapter of his novel with the attempted suicide of the protagonist, who poisons himself.

Towards this aim, Schelin desired to experience the suffering that is usually experienced by suicides.

He got hold of some poison, took it, and then lost consciousness. He was taken from his apartment and placed in Mary Magdalene Hospital. Here he spent about two months.

Having recovered, Schelin resumed writing his "novel."

Now, however, it was required that the protagonist experience the feeling of attempted suicide by drowning.

Today, at two o'clock in the morning, Schelin flung himself from the Tuchkov Bridge into the Little Neva River.

The drowning man was noticed in the nick of time by a river constable and a bridge sentry. They reached Schelin in a lifeboat and pulled him from the water.

In an unconscious state, the "novelist-experimentalist" was placed back in the same Mary Magdalene Hospital. In the morning he regained consciousness.

There's more. Now it's necessary to experience throwing oneself in front of a train. "Only then will all the events of my novel be real and perceptible."

The novelist-tailor's position is a difficult one.

"Shall I read on?" asked Lenochka.

Svistonov nodded his head and closed his eyes.

Novella Thirty-four

A Strange Story

Well, of course, strange things occasionally happen in the courts. Some are so strange you want to laugh until your side splits, and sometimes you want to cry. In one of the latest issues of the Leningrad magazine Judgment, *for instance, a story is related about just such an amusing case from the Akhtyubinskiy Circuit Court.*

A declaration was made to the procurator's office by a certain citizen to the effect that some chap had raped a cow.

At the behest of the procurator, an investigator launched an inquiry into the astounding crime.

An inquest was conducted. The case grew and swelled. The "rapist" was charged, and finally the case along with the indictment fell before the jurisdiction of the Circuit Court.

However, in our penal code no statutes exist by which to sentence such a crime, and the Akhtyubinskiy Court was at a loss.

How to proceed? How to put an end to the matter?

The court got out of this pretty mess quite ingeniously. To bring an action of rape, a declaration from the victim is required—as is written in the law.

You know what the gubernatorial court did?! It dismissed the case— "in view of the absence of a declaration of rape by the victim"...

Lenochka continued.

Novella Thirty-five

The Tattooed Man

On the basis of statutes 846, 847, 848, and 851 of the Regulations Governing Criminal Legal Proceedings, by decision of the Askhabadskiy Circuit Court, from 3 November 1910 Ivan Grigoryev Bodrov, hailing from peasants from the village of Chernyshevo of the Nikolo-Kitskiy District, Karenskiy Region, Penzenskiy Province, is wanted by police and charged with violating statutes 1 and 13 of the penal code.

Features of the accused: 29 years of age, average height, medium build, imposing nature, gray eyes, on his body the following tattoos: 1) drawn on the chest between the nipples is a crucifixion with the inscription "I.N.K.I" on the cross; drawn along the sides of the same are flowers: on the right nipple, a breed of lily; on the left, an unidentifiable breed; 2) drawn beneath the crucifixion to the right and left, on the thorax, are double-headed eagles: on the right half of the thorax, a copy of the Russian national coat of arms with the letter "N" on the band, on the left half of the thorax, a double-headed eagle, not resembling the coat of arms…; 3) depicted on the abdominal area just above the navel and somewhat to the right is a lion with a mane and raised tail; this lion is standing on an arrow whose point faces to the right; 4) depicted along the right side of the lion, of the same height, is Saint George the Victor on a horse defeating a dragon; 5) depicted along the left side of the dragon, of the same height, is a woman (Amazon) sitting on a horse; the head of the horse is facing the lion; 6) depicted on the anterior side of the left arm, above the elbow, is a woman raising the hem of her skirt; 7) depicted on the anterior of the same arm, below the elbow, are unidentified flowers, and below them, a lily;. . . 10) depicted close to the elbow, somewhat lower, is a butterfly, its head facing the above-described flowers; 11) depicted on the anterior side of the right arm, above the elbow, is a woman hitching up her skirt and exposing one leg up to the thigh; 12) below the elbow, on the side of the arm, facing the torso, are depicted an anchor, a cross, and a heart pierced by an arrow; 13) exactly beneath the anchor, heart, and cross is depicted a naked woman standing on some kind of a head and raising a sword with her left hand; 14) depicted to the right of the naked woman with the sword is another woman, half naked and larger in size, her right hand behind her head; 15) to the right of the latter woman is another woman, half naked and holding an opened fan behind her head; 16) depicted to the left of the woman with a sword is a siren with a sword;

17) depicted on the anterior side of the right leg, close to the thigh, is a woman with curly hair, a chain on her neck, no legs, her torso ending in an unintelligible design;

Lenochka blushed.

Svistonov took the book and finished reading himself:

... Anyone to whom the whereabouts of the wanted man is known is obligated to instruct the court as to his location. As for institutions in charge of found property of the accused, they are obligated to immediately hand over such to the supervising board.

Svistonov felt that soon it would be possible to get to work. The novella about the tailor only pricked him like a fleeting insult. The second one went in one ear and out the other. The third one seemed worthy of attention. You could think about that one. Passing the book back to Lenochka and no longer listening to what his wife was reading, he imagined the thirty-fifth novella in the form of a picture.

"The devil only knows," he muttered.

His wife broke off reading and stared at him.

"Andryushenka," she said, "you drank too much again. Don't you feel well?" She went over to the bedding.

"Quickly, a piece of paper," said Svistonov. "Hand me a pencil."

He took the paper and began to draw a naked man.

Svistonov began with the legs, big and muscular, standing on a planked floor, then guided the pencil upward and drew a sturdy torso and hands with trowel-shaped nails. He crowned it all with a nice little head with a smartly twisted mustache.

"Do you have any watercolors?" he asked.

"I think I can find some," Lenochka answered and, after a search, brought them to him.

Svistonov covered the entire image with an even pink hue and, having snatched up the thirty-fifth novella, set about the most important part.

Having selected a thin brush and wetted it with saliva, all the while glancing at the novella, he began drawing symbols in different colors. On the chest between the nipples he placed a silver crucifixion; along the side, a white lily; beneath the crucifixion, he painted a coat of arms and an eagle; on the abdomen, above the navel, he outlined a juicy-looking lion with a mane and a raised tail. He portrayed the skirts as calico; he gave the woman with the fan a circus feel; he reproduced a voluptuous dog and a snake in merry green; and the inscription "God Save Me" he outlined above an indecent place in gold letters ....

The background he covered in black.

Having raised himself on the bed and spat out a fly which had landed in his mouth, Svistonov began looking for a book on the overhead shelf, then below in the night stand. He lit a few of the candles standing in bronze, Empire-style candlesticks. From the night stand he took out a mirror for shaving.

"Lenochka, put some water on," he said.

While Lenochka boiled the water, Svistonov smoked, thoughtfully examining the drawing which he had placed between the candles and the mirror. The black background let in practically no light, and the pink individual came out of a corridor. Svistonov put a non-commissioned officer's uniform on the emerging figure. The coats of arms, the women, the wild beasts were hidden—they were becoming the spiritual and psychological attributes and aspirations of one more manifesting character. Then, having set aside the drawing, he began to shave, contemplating where to go and with whom to become acquainted.

Svistonov entered the House of Publishing. It was a literary evening. A young female author was appearing. After seven years of truly splendid literary activity, which had riveted the cream of society to her as well as to her career, she was pulling a stunt so impermissible and cynical that everyone lowered his eyes and somehow felt an unpleasant physical emptiness. First a man came out leading behind him a toy horse, then some kind of youth pranced around turning cartwheels, then the very same youth, wearing only underpants, rode around the hall on a green childrens tricycle. Behind him appeared Marya Stepanovna.[10]

"Shame on you, Marya Stepanovna!" they yelled at her from the first row. "What do you take us for!"

Not knowing why on earth she was appearing, Marya Stepanovna, in an even voice as if nothing had happened, read her poetry.

Svistonov took a seat in an armchair in the next room. Reclining against the chair's colored back with black caryatids, he tuned his ears into the voices.

A voice in a gray cap was saying that it might be possible to take Cain and Abel in an ironic kind of way.

A voice in blue was relating that he is writing a book of deaths which will be dedicated to Pushkin, Lermontov, Yesenin, and others.

A deep voice in glasses was intoning that people were confusing literary criticism and official administrative measures.

One drinking tea in the next room cried, "I'd like to pay please."

One sitting with his hat in his hand cracked, "A dead man won't squirm."

At intermission Svistonov made his way through the commotion of the crowd to the auditorium.

The public was indignant with the performance.

"So you're not angry with me?" Svistonov asked the exiting Valyavkin.

"I understand, of course, that it's art," he said, throwing up his arms, "but why on earth was a guillotine necessary!"

They forced their way through to the dining room, took seats at a small table by the fireplace.

Svistonov was inspecting the glass of the tumbler he was raising in the air.

"Let us drink," he toasted, "to your future appearance, to your performance. What talent nature has endowed you with!"

Before long, more literary types joined the table, and soon a relaxed and merry gathering had taken shape. Anecdotes alternated with beer; newly written poems, with snarls at reviewers; discussions of recently released books, with those about the ludicrous tendencies of their authors.

All the while, the visiting writer Valyavkin occasionally came to life, then grew sullen again.

He surveyed the dining room.

He had thought they would greet him with open arms, but all the while, as if on purpose, they paid him no attention at all.

"Sure, it's notorious there," said a man at the next table, bursting out in laughter, casting a sidelong glance at the Muscovite. "In Moscow, a fellow giving a reading will come on stage, his chest puffed out, striped stockings showing, arm outstretched, and commence aggrandizing: 'Myself and Shakespeare.' Or else he'll start listing objects, using all his voices, and think it's poetry. You in Moscow live like little canaries, all packed in, while here, we have spatial palaces ..." the speaker was openly addressing the Muscovite. But he was interrupted by another young man, an advertising agent.

"Our men of letters breathe fresh air, dwell in Detskoye Selo, closer to the penates of Pushkin![11] We do real work here. In Moscow you've got loafers."

"Stop, there's no sense arguing about it," calmed the union committee secretary. "Moscow has its merits, and Leningrad's are no less. We do indeed work in peace here, while in Moscow they're restless, but it's still unknown which is better—calm or unrest."

Kuku, sitting at a different table, wanted to go over to where the piano was playing. Kuku was drawn by the piano player, a girl with a gaping mouth, a saddening nose with pimples, and hair that started almost at her eyebrows and had thinned badly from having abortions. With affected grace she was pounding away on the keyboard and singing:

Goodbye, my friend, goodbye. . .

The room seemed quiet to Kuku, and the girl, desirable. However, because spring had not yet set in, his attraction to the girl was not sufficiently strong. But he truly did like the line of her shoulders, shoulders which sloped badly, and the way her fingers rippled in the air and then made little figures on the keys.

Although Kuku was known by everyone, Svistonov had never before paid any attention to him. But now, in the pursuit of material, Svistonov sensed it was imperative to get to know Kuku.

Svistonov polished off his drink and followed Kuku over to the piano, where the girl was singing. Svistonov was surrounded by a crowd of young people laughing.

"Introduce me to Kuku," he said, "I need him for my new character."

Some of the young people broke away and took off.

Ivan Ivanovich Kuku suffered from a strange passion for penning letters. He was a portly forty year-old, had kept himself up superbly. His face was adorned with side-whiskers, his forehead crowned with chestnut hair, and his heartfelt voice at once elicited respect in those he met. "What an intelligent face," they would say. "Such side-whiskers, such pensive eyes. No doubt Ivan Ivanovich is an important man." Ivan Ivanovich felt this. He did his best to attend to his side-whiskers with utmost care. He strove to keep his eyes constantly alight with inspiration and his face ever smiling gently so that everyone would sense he was always thinking of the lofty and the beautiful. He executed everything with grandeur. He shaved with stateliness, smoked with charm, pronounced even trifles with panache: "I should like the beefsteaks today."

"Without doubt I resemble a great man," he thought, stopping occasionally on the street in front of a mirror. Even middle-school students would stare at him and say, "Lookie there, who's that?"

Nothing of Ivan Ivanovich was his own—not his mind, not his heart, not his imagination. Everything in him visited in turns. That of which everyone approved, he approved. He read only those books respected by all. On principle, he did not read other books. He wanted to be of bright mind and worthy soul. He always took up what others took up. When they were taken by religious questions, he was taken by them. When they were inspired by Freudism, he was inspired. His only original character trait was his passion for letters. Ivan Ivanovich loved to write letters and he quivered when he wrote them. They invariably started thus: "I am an honest man and therefore must inform you that you are a cad"; or "You have taken the liberty of spreading vile rumors about a respectable person—you are a scoundrel"; or "You have refused to come by my invitation to the house I recommended to you and show your drawings. I herewith inform you that your drawings are dreadful and only out of mercy for you did I take an interest in them." Receiving such letters, his friends shrugged their shoulders. "Oh, Ivan Ivanovich," they said to one another upon meeting in the street. "We'd better visit him and console him. It's all due to his nerves, you know. My gosh, if we left him, he would be completely alone, and who knows what would happen to him then." They would make arrangements to go, but before they would manage, Ivan Ivanovich, sunken-faced and hunched over, would come to them and apologize.

The acquaintance took place beneath the luminance of chandeliers.

They—Svistonov and Kuku—walked towards each other. They were surprised that, for whatever the reason, they had not been acquainted before. Kuku stated that ever since his youth he had followed Svistonov's career and had wanted to meet the author for some time in order to express his admiration. Svistonov stated that he had heard many delightful and interesting things about Kuku and that it was a pity Kuku didn't write, that if he were to take pen to hand, certainly a most interesting tale would result.

Ivan Ivanovich's soul began to tremble. It seemed to Ivan Ivanovich that he had found a kindred spirit, and he began singing like a swan and posing like a beauty queen before Svistonov. It was as if he were saying to Svistonov, "Look what a mind I have, what extraordinary education. Ah, my friend, my friend! How I suffer! There is hardly anyone for me to converse with. I am surrounded by people who are not the real thing! Ivan Dmitriyevich is a fine fellow, of course, but a nothing when it comes to biology. Dmitriy Ivanovich is not bad on philosophy, but then he's a dreadful person. Konstantin Terentyevich is knowledgeable but never says anything. Terentiy Konstantinovich is talkative but ignorant."

"And have you read this book?" he asked, taking out a book he had only just received. "It completely changed my world view."

They left the House of Publishing together. Kuku was enchanted. Svistonov was gratified. They had agreed to be friends.

Kuku lived on Ligovskiy Prospect in an enormous apartment house, practically a separate city where everything was to be had: a pharmacy, shops, a little park, a bathhouse. Ivan Ivanovich Kuku was the love of his friends. They considered him an unrealized genius. They were astounded by his erudition, they took his flightiness as the scattered nature of a gifted intellect. "Were Ivan Ivanovich to gather up his knowledge and focus it on one point, he would turn the world around," they would say as they parted from Ivan Ivanovich Kuku. And they pitied him terribly.

Spring set in, and Ivan Ivanovich Kuku decided to go for an outing. He took a train, got off at Detskoye Selo, and went by bus to Catherine's Palace, which had been converted into a museum.[12]

Ivan Ivanovich got off at the lyceum, near the entrance.[13] Ivan Ivanovich stood in profile, as he found that his figure benefited from being in this position. He watched the street and made as if reading. From time to time he turned the pages and looked up to see if anyone he knew was around. Meanwhile a crowd was gathering by the lyceum. Several of the people ran up to the statue of Pushkin, studied it carefully, tried to register its features, and returned to their post to share their impressions.

"Of course it looks an awfully lot like him."

"Why, not at all, he doesn't have the same nose."

"But did you look at his forehead?"

"And he does seem to be wearing a waistcoat."

"What kind of hat do you think he's got on?"

Ivan Ivanovich Kuku moved on with his poems by Delvig. The crowd followed behind him at a distance. He passed the statue.

"But what if he's in costume?" whispered a young lady.

"There's an idea! Maybe they're going to shoot a film in the park."

"Quiet, or else everyone will come."

The crowd dwindled. Only the younger ones followed Kuku. He walked past the palace, turned left past the outer buildings, crossed the Chinese footbridge, turned left on the path once more, crossed another bridge to the small island. Kuku loved great individuals with a strange and tender kind of love. He could stand for hours before the portrait of any great man. His soul thirsted for greatness and any kind of uncommon exploit. He loved passionately biographies of great people and was overjoyed when features of his own biography and those of a great person's coincided. After walking along the island, Ivan Ivanovich returned to the lyceum, immodestly and affectedly approached the statue of Pushkin, sat down on a bench, and began gazing at the bronzed adolescent.

All the while, the youths had been standing on the Chinese footbridge waiting for the movie shoot. They dashed out beyond the gate, looked to the left and to the right to see if there might be a car flying by with movie cameras, cameramen, directors, other actors. But clouds of dust on the road did not appear, and soon it was lunch time.

Somewhat disappointed, discussing what it could mean, the young *dachniki* went their separate ways home.[14]

Meanwhile Svistonov was hurrying to the lyceum.

Morning. Svistonov sat on a bench waiting for Kuku while people were still rushing through the park on their way to work. It was cold out, gray, unpleasant. Svistonov got up from the bench and strolled about the park.[15]

The sculpted busts were blackening against a background of trees dressed in rime.

A springless cart was pulling into the Admiralty Gates.

Behind a fence sailors were marching along the carriage way.

A dray was moving off toward the Republican Bridge.

The Palace of Arts, freshly painted in its historical colors, seemed to be whirling off Palace Square.

Angel atop a column, and below him, a floating quadriga, and below that, two storeys and an archway out of which flew an automobile.

Overhead a small aeroplane heading toward the Peter and Paul Fortress was receding in the distance.

At last, from a tram alighted Kuku in a summer hat.

Svistonov walked towards him.

He shook his hand.

Today they were going to the Hermitage Museum. Svistonov wanted to look for representations of hunting.

Kuku wanted to walk through the halls, show himself, watch the people.

"Would you believe," Kuku uttered, "that in childhood I was keenly upset that my nose was not like Gogol's, that I didn't have a limp like Byron, and that I didn't have jaundice like Juvenal."

CHAPTER TWO
TOKSOVO

Slowly the train ascended. Kuku and Svistonov alighted at the station, bought cigarettes, and rattled off in a cabriolet. The cottage had been rented in advance. The windows of the room into which Kuku and Svistonov settled gave onto the road. Other than this room and a log entrance area, there was nothing else to the small cottage. It had been built hastily, specially for *dachniki*. The walls of the room were covered with the cheapest available wallpaper, the table and bunks were made of planks.

The renters did up the walls with the books they had brought. Kuku converted his corner into a study for working. He attached a sheet of dark blue blotting paper to the table with thumbtacks, arranged candlesticks, set down a ream of fresh writing paper. He took out goose feather quills, presented one to Svistonov, kept the other for himself. In the evenings, sitting beside one another, they would work amicably like Goncourts, he inventing the subject and

Svistonov .... Of course it was time. Time for him, Kuku, to get down to work.

On a certain evening a campfire was burning at the foot of one of the hills a few versts from Toksovo. *Dachniki* were lying about in a semicircle, throwing pine branches onto the fire, talking about politics.

May beetles were flying around the young pines.

Grasslands were cut off by the wall of sand below.

Svistonov, a deaf laundress named Trina Rublis, Kuku, and a girl from the city named Nadenka sat among the *dachniki.*

Trina Rublis had a past which was full and wild, and up until recently she had possessed beauty. Some two years ago, though, she had somehow become flabby and unkempt. Her ashen hair no longer provoked poetic comparisons, and her rosy cheeks had turned yellow and puffy.

It was unknown what the creature, living in a world deprived of sounds, was thinking that evening. Perhaps rising in her imagination was a handsome officer of the Wild Division, who after using the passport of a killed comrade to marry her hastily in Detskoye Selo during the Yudenich Offensive on Petrograd, had disappeared without a trace, possibly by no fault of his own.

Kuku sat immodestly at the foot of the other girl, watched the lake ripples over the fire.

Svistonov squeezed the laundress's hand and, having ensured that no one was listening and knowing that she herself would not hear, began telling her a story, toying with the once beautiful deaf girl. She watched his lips and wondered when she was supposed to laugh.

"There, I've brought Kuku and the girl together," continued Svistonov, stroking the deaf girl's hand. "Later I will transport them into another world, more real and everlasting than this momentary life. They will live in it, and by the time they're in their coffins, they will just be starting to live through their prime and change forevermore. Drawing people out of one world and drawing them into another sphere—that is art.

"There aren't many real catchers of souls in the world. Nothing is more formidable than a real catcher. They are quiet, real catchers, and they are polite, for only politeness connects them with the outside world. Of course they don't have snouts or hooves. They pretend to love life, but they love art alone.

"Understand," Svistonov continued, knowing that the deaf girl was not understanding a thing, "art is not pure fanfare, not pure work. It's a fight for the population of another world in order to ensure that that world is fully populated, that it has variety, that it's full of life. Literature might be compared to life beyond the grave. Actually, literature is life beyond the grave."

The fire was burning out. The *dachniki* had gone off to collect brushwood.

Kuku was dozing immodestly at Nadenka's foot.

Svistonov, sitting on a massive tree stump, was conversing with the deaf girl.

Svistonov rose, went over to the couple asleep, sat down next to them. Carefully he studied the lake, the line of a lone bent birch near a precipice, the *dachniki* returning with their brushwood, the sleeping young couple.

"Imagine," he went on, bending forward politely, "a kind of poetic phantom who leads living people to the grave. A kind of Vergilian type among the *dachniki* who in an inconspicuous way leads them to Hell. And the *dachniki,* imagine, with their fingers in their noses and bouquets in their hands, follow him in single file, thinking they're going for an outing. Imagine they see Hell behind some sort of hill. It's a kind of grayish little gully, terribly woeful, and in it they see themselves naked—completely naked, even without their little fig leaves—yet with bouquets in their hands. And imagine that their Vergil down there, also naked, is compelling them to dance to the tune of his fife."

In the twilight Svistonov's voice was growing stronger.

Trina, looking around, couldn't figure out whom Svistonov was angry with.

Now they were descending one hill and climbing another, descending that one and climbing a third. Lakes were on both sides of them as they walked.

The deaf girl signed that she loved the grass and the warmth of the sun on her back.

Turning her head to Svistonov, she touched her back.

It seemed to Svistonov that Trina was getting chilly. He took off his suit jacket and threw it over her shoulders. She smiled, then ran off, glancing back all the while as she went. Svistonov ran after her.

They reached the shore.

"I want to go for a swim," signed the deaf girl.

Turning away, Svistonov walked off and sat down with his back to the lake. Trina Rublis went behind some bushes and undressed. She remained in her blouse only, a blouse held up by two pink ribbons, with a rose embroidered on the breast. She hung her stockings on the bushes.

In her blouse Trina Rublis ran into the lake. She began making noises in the water. Svistonov understood that she wanted him to turn around. Reluctantly Svistonov went down to the water. Visible relatively far from the shore was the deaf girl's head, wrapped in a towel. Then the deaf girl swam toward shore; she lay down near the shoreline, barely being lapped by the water.

Svistonov entered the water wearing his shirt. Taking each other by the hand, they swam.

By the campfire the others had either not noticed their absence or were pretending to have not noticed.

The deaf girl sat closer to Svistonov and fixed her gaze on the flames.

Whether under the influence of the approaching night and coolness or for reasons unrelated, Fedyusha, a reader of poetry and orator, suggested skipping through the fire, but his suggestion was rejected. Then a *kultprosvetchitsa* suggested playing tag.[1]

It was Sunday, and because it was a bright afternoon, countless excursions, preceded by musicians, wended away from the remote, Gothic-style train depot.[2] Trumpets gleamed in the sun. Behind them workers with their wives hurried along. Decked with flowers, they tore off blades of grass or leaves from bushes and chewed.

Other excursions consisted of adolescents in red kerchiefs and youngsters wearing swimming trunks and carrying their sandals in their hands. Still others—of students who had been compelled to stay in the city for one reason or another. Every procession had been supplied with a placard and a group leader wearing an arm band.

On such days, the Russian Switzerland Tavern came to life.

At the tables it grew noisy. People clinked steins, hugged, ate ice cream, guffawed, ran from one table to another, ate cucumbers, cottage cheese, eggs with sausages, sucked on fruit drops taken from their pockets or reticules. Here and there someone let out a "Yaa-hoo!"

By two o'clock the hills above the lake came to life as well. The orchestra situated itself between two or three pines on the very top of a hill. Crowds swam in knickers of various colors and, lying on their stomachs, bathed in the sun. And again from afar someone let out a "Yaa-hoo!" and it carried across the hills.

The Toksovo highlands transformed into living mountains of humanity, and the placards, when swaying in the wind, looked like banners and pennants and glittered in the sun with their white, yellow, black, and golden letters.

Withered Tanya and withered Petya stepped outside. Petya locked the door and ran his fingers over the lock.

"Here we are again, in the bosom of nature. It's been ten years since we've been to the dacha. Did you grab the magazines and newspapers? It's nice to read lying under the shade of a tree."

"You're your old self," Tanya fell gaily into revelry, putting on gloves and opening her long parasol with its lace and its bone handle.

They set out directly across a field to the lake. Tanya wore a shortish checked skirt, which gave young people the chance to make fun of her crooked legs, and a low-necked crêpe de Chine blouse adorned with a slightly bedraggled light blue ribbon.

"The sun's warming up," Tanya said.

"Indeed," confirmed Petya.

"Oh look, flowers!" Tanya bent down.

"They're buttercups," added Petya. "My young little thing, you!"

"I'm off!"

Tanya started off along the path, began bending down, picking flowers, weaving a wreath out of little branches. Petya sat down on a stump and opened a newspaper. Petya's face was all in wrinkles. His back was stooped, his eyes short-sighted.

Tanya sang a romance and, weaving a sprig, walked slowly down into a vale.

Her aged hands fairly swiftly picked clover, chamomile, bluebells. Her shriveled little legs trod almost confidently over the grass.

"It's nice here, Tanya," she heard his jingling voice from above.

And once again silence.

Only the newspaper above rustled.

Below noiselessly fluttered butterflies. Gray hair came undone from beneath her light blue hat. Tanya laughed. Ah, youth, youth! She spread out a handkerchief, sat down on it, removed the hat, and placing the wreath on her head, listened to the grass buzzing, singing, hissing.

In the mornings, by old habit, Tanya sponged Petya down. A husband, what a fuss! She actually stood the spindly dear old man in a basin with water and sponged him down.

At one time Petya had played flute in the Academic Theater. He had played with feeling, and Tatyana Nikandrovna had sat somewhere in the theater with a girlfriend and listened.

Up above, Petya, having put his newspaper on the grass, removed his flute from its case and played.

Svistonov, strolling above the shoreline of the lake and observing the holiday crowd, heard the flute.

The couple had a dog. She was like a child to them. A fine little nine year-old fox terrier who had aged so quickly and imperceptibly. Yes, as in the past, she still had a pink ribbon around her neck, and as in the past, she still ran along the ground, her face lowered, but by now the couple no longer called her Traviata, but simply "old girl."[3] And so the old girl with her pink bow sat beside the old man expectorating into his flute, while below, another old girl with a light blue bow, hair cropped, a wreath on her head, lay with a green leaf in her mouth and watched the sky.

The little fox terrier came running. She sat beside the old woman and peered into the grass, as if dozing off.

Svistonov walked along, parting the bushes with a stick.

The deaf girl walked affectedly, crooking her neck.

The old man played more and more spiritedly.

For some time Svistonov gazed down from the hill and listened to the flute. Then he descended.

"Allow me to introduce myself," he said. "Andrey Svistonov."

"Very pleased to meet you." The old man, having been taken unawares, set down his flute and bustled about.

The deaf girl stood a ways off.

"You play marvelously," commenced Svistonov. "I love music. I've been wanting to meet you for some time."

The old man blushed.

"In the evenings I hear you playing ...."

Taking a stroll around the lake, Svistonov and Kuku came across Nadenka, walking in the company of the Telyatnikov brother and sister. Nadenka was making her way slowly, playing with a twig, brother and sister on either side of her. There was twenty year-old Pasha, who considered himself an aged man and principally said clever things, and seventeen year-old Iya, a know-it-all. Pasha was pensive and sullen, as he was under the impression that he was from bad lineage and had been ill-disposed since infancy. Iya was exuberant and spoke about Anatole France. Sister and brother were friends with Nadenka and hated each other.

Upon seeing Svistonov and Kuku, the Telyatnikovs bowed and went to say hello.

"Andrey Nikolayevich," Iya said, "what a new anecdote I have to tell you!" And she set off next to Svistonov to his right.

Kuku, Nadenka, and Pasha followed behind. Pasha considered Svistonov a major talent. Thus he looked on with envy as Svistonov conversed with Iya. Pasha was overjoyed when Svistonov, turning halfway around, continuing to walk, addressed him. Immediately the youth caught up and set off along the other side. Brother and sister had aspirations.

Kuku and Nadenka dropped behind.

"How about a game of *gorodki*?" Svistonov proposed as the dachas in the distance came into view.[4]

Pasha didn't feel right refusing, although he considered it a worthless and loathsome pastime. Iya assented with glee and ran off to procure sticks and small stumps from a ditch. Svistonov took a stick and began outlining boundaries of *gorodki*. Up above, on a hilltop, appeared Kuku and Nadenka.

Svistonov started out towards them.

"We're getting ready to play *gorodki*," he said. "Would you care to join in?"

Kuku declined.

"A singular person, that Svistonov," pronounced Kuku, holding Nadenka by the elbow as they made their way down to the lake. "What zeal in him, what cheer, what ingenuity. From appearances, he loves Toksovo. To me it doesn't appeal at all. Nature here doesn't stir the spirit, the emotions. I like to live where everything is grand. It's good to live in the company of great people, to converse with great people."

"Oh stop, Ivan Ivanovich." Nadenka raised her eyes. "Look how nice it is here."

Her eyes were charming indeed. Half green, half hazel.

In the heavens that evening were a fleece of clouds, and in the lake, both azure and a fleece of waves.

Kuku covered a stump with his coat. Nadenka sat down.

Kuku sat below her.

"Nadenka," he said lovingly, "this evening troubles me.

Wasn't it on just such an evening that Prince Andrey beheld Natasha at the ball and enshrined her in his memory? Do you like Natasha?"

Nadenka smoked dreamily, followed the rings as they dissipated into the air.

"Why do you smoke, Nadenka?" Kuku asked. "It doesn't fit your image in the least. Inside you there must be great vitality and naturalness. Quit smoking, Nadenka." Distress was in Kuku's voice.

Nadenka tossed her cigarette. The cigarette fell on dry turf and continued to smolder and smoke.

The girl was quiet. "But I'm getting ready to become a movie actress, you know."

"Nadenka, it's not possible," muttered Kuku.

"Why isn't it possible, Ivan Ivanovich?"

"If you trust me, don't make that step. Believe in my experience. You must be Natasha!"

Above them appeared Svistonov with the sister and brother. Svistonov sat down with Iya beneath a tree. Pasha commenced reading poems to the writer.

"Marvelous," said Svistonov. "Talented."

Pasha beamed.

"So it's worthwhile to write?" he asked.

"Of course it's worthwhile!" confirmed Svistonov and looked below, thinking that it was time to go. "Would you be so kind," he said to Iya, "as to ask Ivan Ivanovich what time it is."

Iya rushed away at a gallop.

At that moment Ivan Ivanovich was admiring the lake. Iya appeared and, smiling, asked the pensive figure, "Do you have the time?"

Kuku took out his watch.

"Ten," he answered solidly. "Where's Svistonov?"

"Waiting up there."

Iya made her way over to Nadenka.

"Were you bored?" she asked quietly.

Now it was a threesome walking—Svistonov, Nadenka, and Kuku. The Telyatnikovs followed behind.

"Don't you think," asked Pasha sullenly, "that Svistonov was intentionally playing *gorodki* with us so that Kuku could woo Nadenka?"

"Cut it out, please," answered Iya. "Where do you get such suspicion? Svistonov simply likes young people."

Again it was Sunday. Cabriolets were parked near the church.[5] Inside, the church was filled with yellow-haired young men and with young ladies resembling paper roses. The organ played. Light fell through the stained glass. Nadenka and Kuku were standing up above. Behind them were Svistonov and Trina Rublis. Nadenka and Kuku watched the christening below, occasionally cast their glance toward the aisle and saw a bride, bridegroom, and escorts preparing to move to the altar as soon as the christening was over.

The bridegroom was anxious and shifted from one foot to another. The bride was red as a crayfish.

"What material for us, Andrey Nikolayevich," Kuku, leaning back, said into Svistonov's ear. "Fix it in your mind, I beg you, fix it!" And Kuku again took to watching.

The blonde hair on the back of Nadenka's head stirred Kuku, and he imagined his wedding. Pride was written all over Kuku's face. He saw himself standing next to Natasha—that is, next to Nadenka. Nadenka in a white dress and a veil. In her hands, a candle with a white bow, and the echoing vaults of the cathedral…

Having taken out a handkerchief, Kuku immodestly wiped his face.

The deaf girl was reminiscing about Riga—what a beautiful city, Riga—and the hopes she had had and the walk to the woods she had taken with a vacationing student named Toropov.

But Kuku disrupted her reminiscences. He let out a cough, constrained his chest. Now he looked on disdainfully. Below, the young couple started. Everyone in the church stirred. All heads turned toward the aisle. Svistonov watched too.

The organ played. Then the pastor spoke. Then the organ played once more.

Through the stained glass, leaves on the trees could be seen flickering, lit by the sun.

"Very nice," Kuku uttered. "But I should like greater splendor for my wedding."

Nadenka, Kuku, Svistonov, and the deaf girl left the church. Back flew the cabriolets.

"Let's drop in for some beer," suggested Kuku. Dipping into the crowd, they entered a garden adjacent to a tavern. All the tables and benches were occupied. Laughter and the heavy odor of beer. Wafts of smoke, flushed faces, songs, the sounds of balalaikas, guitars, and mandolins.

"A genuine open-air Auerbach Tavern," said Kuku to Svistonov. "All we need is Faust and Mephistopheles."

"Come now, Ivan Ivanovich," retorted Svistonov, "always literary recollections. You ought to approach life more simply, more directly."

A table at last became free. The four friends sat down and called for beer. By this time the brother and sister had jostled their way over to them.

"May we sit down?" they asked and squeezed in somehow at the end of the bench.

"I know how to drink," said Iya after her fifth glass, "but as for you, Pasha, even though you're a man, you don't."

"I know how to drink," Pasha answered, "but I contain myself."

"I've got a funny anecdote!"

"Your anecdotes are of no interest to me."

"And your poetry, to me!"

"Don't quarrel," begged Nadenka.

At the next table, lively conversations were going on:

"As to the Germans, brother, you're mistaken. When the Germans had me in captivity..."

"That dame's not bad. I'm going after her."

"Where you going? You're loaded. Sit down!"

On the left:

"No, not at all! Mitya, look what a fanny! Masha, Masha, come over here."

On the right, beneath the pine trees:

"Indeed, Petya, culture is a great word. Ivan Trofomovich told me people have gone to the stake for it."

"Oh sure, you'll help achieve culture. Drink up, buffoon."

"Mitka, I've seen the light, I go to church now. Just don't tell anybody, all right? Nobody."

A voice from the crowd waiting for tables:

"Volodya! Volodenka! Go take your nap in the dump!"

A drunk, teetering, yells out:

"Get over here, I'll belt you one!"

Behind the fence a group of guys shows up. They lead a girl by the wrists, little boys prancing around them. The girl's dress is rumpled, her hair disheveled. Crying bitter tears, she yells out:

"Ooh, I feel sick, I feel oh so sick! Oh, let me do my hair!" She tries to break free. The guys, laughing, twist her arms. She tries to fling herself onto the ground, but held under the arms by her smirking assailants, sinks down.

"She was sleeping in the bushes with some guy," the boys explain to the crowd. "We're taking her to the police."

"No, no... You're not Natasha, you're Gretchen," whispers a drunk Kuku. "And I'm Faust. And Svistonov's Mephistopheles. And the deaf girl, Marta!"

"Don't talk nonsense," interrupts Svistonov, perturbed.

An old worker, plodding heavily, approaches the table of friends.

He halts, staggers.

"You, educated people, one can ask you what..."

Kuku, excited, brushes Svistonov with his elbow.

In a whisper:

"It's the scene behind the city gates," he says jubilantly. "Next he'll call me doctor!"

The worker looks into Kuku's face, contemplating.

"Citizen, if I may be so bold as to ask... you wouldn't be a doctor?"

Kuku laughs smugly.

Svistonov and the deaf girl, Kuku and Nadenka, and Pasha and Iya had agreed to take a pleasure trip to the country. They set off to a remote lake, taking with them blankets, cushions, canned meats, cigarettes, and a little cognac.

The sun was just lighting the hilltops when they set out. It had rained the day before, and a whitish fog was running down from the hills to the lakes. The sky was blue, though, and sparrows chirped and flew up to the dampened leaves covered with glistening droplets, swung on the sprigs, flew down to the road winding into the distance. The ditches on the side of the road, itself drying up and turning more yellow by the hour, were full of water.

Iya made good money and was wearing yellow boots, a foreign coat bought secondhand, and a yellow portfolio with straps. She had purchased cognac, a head of Dutch cheese, a tin of fresh caviar, and a few jars of fruit drops and compote. She walked in the lead carrying a green bag behind her back.

Pasha hadn't bought anything but was under Nadenka's patronage. She had loaded him up with a pillar of her favorite cookies, jelly-filled pies, a blanket, a small pillow, a towel, soap, a mug, and a toothbrush. The deaf girl carried sweet cheese tarts and cutlets.

Kuku had been terrific. Specially for the outing, he had dashed into town and retrieved leather boot tops, purchased a gray cap, and donned a mackintosh. He walked along gaily carrying an actor's case. In the case, side by side with Pushkin, lay a veal, a roast beef, knives, forks, a stack of cups, a bottle of French wine.

Svistonov had not sloughed off either. He carried a collapsible tent, a mirror, a camera.

Svistonov made like he was paying court to the deaf girl. He was interested to see what kind of gossip would arise.

He bowed and presented her with flowers picked by the ditches.

Nadenka turned around in surprise.

Kuku, not wishing to be outdone by Svistonov, also plucked some flowers and, tying them into a bouquet, presented them to Nadenka.

Pasha ran far off into a field and brought back cornflowers by the bunch.

"Can you whistle?" Svistonov asked Iya. "Go ahead, whistle."[6]

Iya commenced virtuoso whistling.

"In step," proposed Svistonov, "let's walk in step."

Kuku, smiling, shifted his leg.

Nadenka asked how it was done.

Kuku demonstrated.

They walked thus to the nearest village. Iya whistled the fox-trot.

They approached the village. Milk maidens and children watched and wondered where they were heading in such military fashion. Feeling the curious gazes upon themselves, the procession smiled.

"Keep in step," Svistonov said. "Louder, Iya! Louder!"

"Perhaps we should have a little something to eat?" Kuku suggested suddenly.

"I'm hungry as a wolf," said Iya, turning her head around.

"And you, Nadenka?"

"With pleasure."

"To the pine tree. It's shady there and cool and perfectly dry."

"Hand me my case," Nadenka asked.

Pasha handed it to her.

Iya threw down her green bag and began rummaging through it.

Kuku opened his case and began taking out knives, forks, cups.

"To think that only a few years ago," said Kuku, "there were wolves around Petersburg."[7]

"Really?" asked Nadenka.

"We all thought that everything was over then, but here we are eating and drinking, and things are just like before."

"You think so?" asked Svistonov and smiled.

"Yesterday I read a new biography of Napoleon and regretted that I wasn't of small stature."

Iya was uncorking a bottle. Ivan Ivanovich tried in vain to take the corkscrew away from her. Nadenka sliced the roast beef and the veal. She had been unanimously elected hostess.

Nadenka sincerely was enjoying herself.

Once everyone was full, Kuku took out Turgyenev's correspondence with Dostoyevskiy and began reading, but the picnickers, fatigued from the food, began dozing while sitting up.

A room with two windows appears to Nadenka. It's bright, there's sun outside. Near one window sits a young woman. Stooping over her is a man, tall, gaunt, with a repulsive face, balding between long, straight hair. Especially repulsive are the eyes on his gray face. They're boring into her somehow. He is dressed in a dirty brown suit from the sixteenth century, something from one of those historical films. She knows he is the master of her fate and that he will do with her, Nadenka, whatever he wants, and she is dreadfully afraid of him.

She starts running through endless rooms. A gigantic house like a labyrinth. The man alone lives in it. She runs through a hallway, again through bright rooms, through a living room with stuccoed walls. Sometimes at the end of a hallway she catches sight of him. He laughs, delighting in her fright, and she again runs, realizing all the time that he can see her and find her. Finally she runs into a room like a kitchen; she knows that here a door leads outside. She looks at the wall and at once understands why the man knows where she is: on the wall is a floor plan of the house, and on it is a thin copper wire showing Nadenka's entire path while at the same time lying itself down in her trail, showing all along where she's headed. There's a small free end of the wire, and Nadenka sees herself peeling it back and bending it upward. Now she knows the wire won't show anything.

She runs outside. All the buildings are under construction. They're only tall shells, six storeys and higher, with gigantic openings for windows, two floors in height. On the street are piles of dirt, lime, ballast.

Amidst the buildings stands one that's finished, but it's far off. A light is visible there, and she decides to run to it.

She goes along, stumbling past the unfinished buildings and their foundation pits, farther, farther. In front of her it's completely dark, like in a mine, and sharp iron rods stick out like bristles. She's lost! The buildings are buckling; she's afraid they'll soon crumble. She sees a light.

A young man is walking towards her, and all the while behind him the light is reflecting like a path. He has a very fine face. She runs to him and tells him about running out of the labyrinth. When she tells him that she turned up the end of the wire, his face becomes exultant. He takes her in his arms and, stepping very lightly, carries her toward the light. Then he carries her to the large house and says, "We are going to live here. I know a room, and even though the labyrinth is right next to it, he will never guess to look so close."

All around people are running and bustling, but no one is paying them any attention. And they walk through dark corridors where light is barely discernible, like in paintings by Dutch masters....

Nadenka flinched, woke up, and looked around. Kuku was sitting beneath a large pine tree, browsing through a book. Svistonov, leaning against a tree, was standing and watching her. She felt uneasy.

Pasha was lying down, his knees bent. He was flying in an abyss, and in the abyss his big toe was swelling up, and an abscess was appearing, turning into an eye. It was a revolting sight, and he woke up. He rubbed his eyes with his fists, touched his feet. He yawned.

"I had a silly dream," Pasha said, "that an eye was growing on my foot. Ivan Ivanovich, they say that you know about dreams."

"You know how to interpret dreams?" Nadenka livened up.

"Well, here's a topic for conversation," thought Kuku and responded solidly:

"In ancient times they attached great significance to dreams. There even existed an entire science, if you can call it a science, called oneiromancy. The ancient world never doubted that dreams arise in the soul by divine power." Kuku, satisfied with his knowledge, looked at the others to see if they were listening and how they were listening. "Therefore," he continued, "from this point of view, a dream has significance. However, if to note the hour at which the dream occurred as well as the fact that earlier we ate quite heartily, then your dream, Nadenka, is not completely reliable."

Kuku surveyed his listeners triumphantly and, in order to command even more of Nadenka's respect, decided to invoke Apuleius.

"According to Apuleius, an aftereffect of abundant food is dark and foreboding dream activity," he pronounced bombastically. "Furthermore, oneirocritics confirm that the residual vapors of spirit, even in the morning, impede seeing the truth in dreams. Now, Nadenka, by no means do I agree with this, although I do not know your dream." He spread his arms.

"Perhaps you might relate to us what you saw in your dream? It's quite fascinating. And I, for my part, will bring in the dreams of great individuals, and we can spend the time till sundown in reminiscences. Yes, I'll recount to you the dreams of great individuals.... Ah, I've just now begun to see how beautiful it is here, hills all around....

And having forgotten that Nadenka had yet to relate her dream, Kuku began pensively:

"Above all, we should turn to..."

Iya and Pasha came closer and stood still. Nadenka,

though, was dispirited and didn't listen closely. Dreams of great individuals did not interest her. Although her dream had turned out quite happily, all around it nevertheless had grown dark, even chilly. And indeed, during their after-lunch rest, rain clouds had blanketed sky.

Rumbling in the distance.

They gathered their things and moved them to the base of the pine tree. Svistonov, with the help of the brother and sister, set up the tent. Everyone got in and moved his things from the pine tree.

"Well, why isn't it raining?" joked Ivan Ivanovich.

"Just wait, Ivan Ivanovich," interrupted Iya. "I head the nature section of the *Red Gazette*. I'm a specialist on weather."

In the tent it was dark. Svistonov lit up.

"Andrey Nikolayevich, don't smoke," said Nadenka indignantly. "It's stifling in here."

Svistonov threw out his cigarette.

"Pasha, don't you dare! Get away!" ordered Nadenka.

"Nadenka, this is the perfect time," pronounced Kuku. "It's dark, a storm is brewing. We all promise to listen to you carefully."

The thunderstorm moved off.

Alone, supporting himself against the trunk of the pine tree, Pasha smoked. He was contemplating Nadenka's kiss. Had it been brotherly or not brotherly? Most likely only brotherly. Too light, too airy. "She doesn't love me," he thought. "She can't fall in love with me. For her to love me, I'd have to be outgoing, plus I don't have any kind of future. I'll finish the institute, teach geography." He burst out with laughter. "So be it, but I will not work for the newspapers. Let Iya make her money. Then again, Nadenka does like the theater, sweets, the cinema...."

"Daydreaming?" Nadenka asked, approaching along the trail from behind. "It's nice to dream. I'll sit down, and you lay your head on my knee and keep dreaming. I'll imagine that I'm the heroine of a film, a well-experienced woman, and you're an unhappy young man in love. I'll stroke your head."

Pasha obediently lay down on the grass and laid his head on the fringe of Nadenka's dress.

"I love you," he said softly. "I truly love you."

"Wonderful," Nadenka interrupted. "More suffering now.... Yes, that's it.... Oh, my darling!" She lowered her face and pressed her hand to his heart. "I believe you suffer! How sad it is that we met so late, when I already love another! So he is worthless, so he is depraved.... With matters of the heart," she sighed deeply, "there is nothing you can do. But you are pure, you are delicate, you are only—"

"Nadenka!" Pasha groaned.

"Kiss my hands and cry, then get up and go over to the edge of the cliff. I'm coming," muttered Nadenka, doing her best not to open her lips.

Pasha obediently stood up, kissed her hand, slowly ambled over to the cliff.

Nadenka sat, watched, then ran and cried out, doing her best to run glamorously:

"Arnold, Arnold!"

"You're a doll, Pasha," she said. "Let me give you a kiss."

Pine branches rustled, berries gleamed red on wild rose bushes. The former anarchist Ivanov headed up the hill. He was of average size, pale in the face, shaggy. He trudged along, leaning on a stick, lowered himself onto a bench by the front garden.

At the dacha, not far from the lake, Zoya Znobishina came out onto the porch, yawned, put her hands behind her neck and, raising her head, pointed her elbows out and yawned again. She sat down in the soft rocking chair and examined her hands. Then she turned her head to the right, toward the garden, and yawned once more. She watched with interest as the cat sneaked up on a pigeon. She paced around the porch, went out into the garden, and realized the sun was sweltering, it was time to get dressed.

In the neighboring dacha, up on the hill, local mothers were having a heartfelt conversation about their children playing nearby. Of course their children would be engineers; they already had unusual talent for their ages. One already was whistling like a locomotive. Another was dreaming about a submarine.

Zoya Znobishina came out onto the porch once more. She tightened her shawl and then loosened it again. Chewed on her lips. Everything now was so dull! She started off, chewing on her lips, making zigzags along the path. Ivanov stood up, bowed.

"Bored?" Zoya asked and sat down beside him. "Life's hard on you.

"Yeah, well..." she continued, "life ain't but a little tin lying in the road."

Crossing her legs and raising them, Zoya looked up at Ivanov. "I like people like Svistonov. He's a fun sort."

"He's unscrupulous."

"You envy him," Zoya decided.

"Enough about your Svistonov."

"Just you wait. Wait, I'll introduce you to him, and he'll do a character sketch of you. He'll look you over for a while and describe you. You're good material for him. He loves little ghosts."

"Zoya Fyodorovna, I'm no little ghost."

"You're lying, you are so a little ghost." She chewed on her lips. "I'm bored."

Zoya Fyodorovna's birthday rolled around.

She didn't hide her years well. Rosy, rouged, with recently dyed hair, she awaited her guests.

Scheduled to arrive were Pavlusha Uronov, a stage actor; Allochka Bazykina, the "little bird," as they called her to her face as well as behind her back; Vanya Galchenko, a cultured young man; Senya Ipatov, an unaccomplished singer. They were all very interesting people. At least that was the opinion they had of one another.

In the morning Petya the ice cream man had been told to come with his cart at five o'clock so that there would be ice cream immediately after dinner. In the morning Zoya and the housemaid had cleaned raspberries. Ivanov had helped them. In the morning the delivery men had all shown up: one had brought cream cheese and sour cream, another, mushrooms, another, fish.

First to arrive was Vanya Galchenko, the cultured young

man. He brought a 19th century fantasia, purchased at the flea market. The fantasia depicted a vase, apparently Pompeian.

"Oh, I can't, I can't." Zoya Fyodorovna waved her arms. "Can't you see I'm cleaning raspberries."

"That's okay," Vanya replied, seizing and kissing her bare elbow. "Happy birthday!" And he placed his package on the commode.

"Sit in the garden for now, I'll be finished soon."

Vanya went into the garden and took a seat on the bench. His face was unremarkable, his forehead, smallish. There was a rather droopy, not-well-rested look to Vanya. He had extremely short eyelashes. He was dressed in a faded blue suit, and his tie stuck out from under his vest. Vanya could play some piano, sing a bit, dance. After reading Kurbatov, he loved St. Petersburg and its environs.[8] With nothing to do from 1918 to 1924, he had visited museums. Now he worked somewhere.

Having sat a while and grown bored, Vanya went out the gate, down to the road, and turning his head to the Gothic-style train station, waited for the guests.

Dust clouded the roadway, and the head of a horse appeared. The horse clambered up the hill, leading forth a cabriolet carrying Pavlusha Uronov and the "little bird."

Vanya Galchenko ran over, helped Allochka Bazykina out, and extended his greetings.

"Well, how are you? What's new?" he asked, hoping not to hear anything new.

Telling them about the weather and the train and how

dusty it was in town, Vanya escorted the guests to the porch. He again headed down to the road and once more took to walking alongside the ditches, wearing a knotted handkerchief instead of his cap.

The day's guest were almost assembled. They were sitting on benches and on beechnut chairs brought from inside and playing a game of forfeits when, completely unexpectedly, appeared Psikhachyov, a collector of foul things, as he liked to crack wise about himself.

He saluted Zoya Fyodorovna, who had come out onto the veranda, with hand as well as words: "You see, I have not forgotten that today is your birthday. Albeit without invitation, I have arrived." This was a rather corpulent, older individual, yellow in the face, with slightly curly gray hair, slovenly dressed to the utmost degree. His trousers were frayed at the ends, his vest was covered with grease stains.

Having said hello, Zoya Fyodorovna again left to tend to her hostess duties.

All the while the guests were passing along a handkerchief and making proclamations, every so often getting on their knees, doing their best not to soil their clothes. Vanya Galchenko's dark blue casque, having been placed on a separate chair, was filling up little by little. In it, pencils, penknives, brooches, rings, and a little notebook gleamed in the sun.

The housemaid, leaning out the porch door, gleefully watched the merrymakers. Plump, jovial, rouged, barefooted, she loved Zoya Fyodorovna's guests, always so polite and courteous. She watched them blindfold Pavlusha Uronov, respectable and resisting, and sit him down on a chair. Meanwhile bald-headed Senya Ipatov held the casque filled with small items, and the little bird, standing on tip-toes, pulled out a pencil in a silver case and asked in a delicate voice, gasping with laughter, what to do with this forfeit. Having thought it over, Pavlik Uronov, giving his voice a sepulchral character, pronounced, "Spin around on one leg." And the tousled housemaid watched on as, over by the flower box where a round, pink metal lawn ornament stood, Vanya Galchenko, lifting one foot and folding his arms in front of his chest, began spinning.

"More, more," they all cried, clapping. And he spun faster and faster. The little bird selected a notebook from the hat and once more asked, laughing impassionedly, "And what to do with this forfeit?"

Again Pavel Uronov gave some thought and, raising his hands as high as he could, proclaimed, "Feed the pigeons."

Craning her neck, Dasha could see the guests arranging the chairs in a single row and then sitting down and turning their heads ever so quickly.... and she could see that Kuku kissed Nadenka.

After dinner, the evening public, that is the *dachniki*, began to assemble. The air was getting cool, and Zoya Fyodorovna handed out to the guests her warm things. The ladies got a shawl, jacket, and scarf. Over Uronov's shoulders she draped a raspberry velvet cardigan, set aside for altering and therefore brought from the city.

The talent show began.

Uronov recited:

The devil swings the swing
With his hairy hand....[9]

He declaimed loudly and brilliantly, his navy suit standing out nicely against the background of natural greenery.

Pasha, hesitating, read his poetry.

The little bird performed a music hall number about a clown.

Psikhachyov, resting his leg on the crosspiece of the fence, conversed with Svistonov.

"I'm an interesting model for you, you know. Make me a main character. I've punched out an Austrian prince. Women chase after me. They're just a bunch of aphids over there. Why tinker around with them?" He looked at the guests. "I'm another matter. Are you listening? Do you want me to tell you fetid stories about all of them? Okay? But don't forget me. Definitely put me in. Take out your notebook and write this down."

Svistonov, smiling, took out his tidy little notebook.

"I'm a doctor of philosophy. Don't believe it? You're free to describe me with all my drooling and fetid stories. Yes, I'm ambitious. Tell me, are you talented? Are you a genius? You'll portray me well. I want everybody's finger pointing at me. Leave the surname as it is—Psikhachyov.[10] It rings proud."

"And women really chased after you?" asked Svistonov, smiling.

"I'll tell you. A lake, Switzerland—you know, that kind of nonsense. I was a student, and I tormented her against a backdrop of mountains. I tormented her but I didn't take her."

"You couldn't?" asked Svistonov.

"I like to torment women."

"That's old hat, it won't do for a novel."

Svistonov, having put down his little book, played with his pencil, fastened to his pocket by a silver chain.

"Let's try approaching you in a different way," he said. "You're... a quiet, simple man, a lover of the small things in life. You're not taken by global problems because you know you can't deal with them. The curiosity inside you isn't artistic, but rather womanly. You've attended philosophy lectures out of curiosity and studied botany out of curiosity...."

"Yes, you know I even entered the university just so I could revile it. Without any kind of conviction I studied and even received a doctorate just so I could laugh at philosophy."

"Inside you there's something not of this world," Svistonov joked.

"My life is passing in vain, my artistically constructed life!" Psikhachyov exclaimed woefully. "I'm unable to write about myself. If I were able, I wouldn't have come to you."

"It's all romance," said Svistonov, hiding his pencil. "Tell me something more interesting."

"Like hell it's romance!" Psikhachyov, drawing his face closer to Svistonov's, gushed with drool. "A person lives his whole life with the desire to revile everything but is unable to do so. He hates all people but is unable to disgrace them! He can see they all despise him yet is unable to expose them for what they are. If I possessed your talent, oh yes, I would have all of them under my thumb! Under my thumb, I tell you! So you see, it's a tragedy."

"It's a mere turn of events, dear Vladimir Yevgenyevich, not a tragedy."

In the background rang out:

In stony caves diamonds couldn't be counted....

Psikhachyov was silent. And Svistonov was silent.

It was growing dark.

Silhouettes, moving slowly and embracing one another, could be seen in the windows of the brightly lit house.

"Really, aren't I more interesting, in your opinion, than these people?" Svistonov's interlocutor cut short the silence.

"That's all nonsense. Every person is interesting to me in his own way."

"I'm not asking about that. Not to you, but in general."

Zoya Fyodorovna came into view on the porch, then in the garden. Taking note of the approaching white figure, Svistonov uttered hastily:

"Give me your address." And he wrote it down in the darkness.

Zoya Fyodorovna appeared before the silent pair. "What are you standing here for? You're dancing, aren't you?" she addressed Psikhachyov.

Psikhachyov bowed.

"I'm dancing, Zoya Fyodorovna, dancing."

Entering the house, they bumped into Nadenka in the doorway and behind her, Kuku, moving rhythmically to the music.

"Where you off to?"

"We're danced out. We're going to the garden to get some fresh air," answered Nadenka, gasping for breath.

"All right, but make sure you come back soon."

Nadenka and Kuku sat down on the bench.

"The moon," Kuku began, "it's... romance. Although in these sober-minded times there's no place for romance.... nonetheless, Nadenka, the insidiousness of human nature is such that the moon acts on me. Remember, remember..."

He moved a branch aside and continued:

"the myriad legends, the tales of antiquity. For now I feel like speaking, with the music as my guide, Nadenka, about fatal twins, about evil knights, about a beautiful townswoman! How I would like to live in those distant times. I see myself in a Gothic castle at the proverbial midnight hour...."

In an elucidating whisper:

"Midnight. And my twin. He is tall, pale as ash. He beckons me to follow him. The bridge lowers by itself, chains rattling. We emerge onto a dark field, and there my twin throws down the gauntlet, and we battle, and how I suffer.... For in my castle so high is my young bride, alone in an abandoned bed. It's you, Nadenka!"

"A stupendous film!" replied Nadenka. "What a pity the music stopped!"

"Oh, Nadenka, Nadenka," pronounced Kuku, "be the wax in my hands. What a person I will create of you! We will live so quietly.... No, rather, we'll travel. We'll visit notable countries, behold monuments, and I'll become famous.... It's just that I'm terribly lazy...."

"I won't give up the cinema." Nadenka shook her head.

"Why, even for me, you wouldn't give it up?" asked Kuku, doing his best to speak jovially.

"Look, there's Pasha."

Pasha was standing on the brightly lit porch looking for Nadenka in the darkness of the garden.

Kuku and Nadenka sat still.

"What an unpleasant fellow," said Kuku quietly.

Pasha, having stood a while, unresolvedly went back inside.

The crowd was dispersing noisily, unsteadily.

Svistonov walked through the gate with Ivanov.

"They've been talking about you, saying you're an unpleasant fellow."

"Idle gossip," answered Svistonov, taking Ivanov under the arm. "Being a writer is not particularly pleasant," he continued. "One must not show too much, but then, not too little."

"Most of all, he shouldn't cause people grief," remarked Ivanov.

"Of course," replied Svistonov. "What a still night tonight! What a delightful fellow, that Ivan Ivanovich Kuku! Utterly delightful aspirations! An uncommon affectation for great individuals! Have you known him long?" he asked Ivanov.

"About five years."

"Tell me, how would you explain the fact that he..."

It was early in the morning by the time Svistonov and Ivanov returned to the dacha. Zoya Fyodorovna was still asleep amidst the chaos of various objects, papers, mounds of cigarettes butts, presents.

She was luxuriating in her bed and sighing.

"So," she asked Ivanov at dinner, "how did you like Svistonov?"

"Charming fellow."

"Well, you just wait."

With each day Kuku became more convinced that Nadenka was Natasha, and there appeared in him a strength of will, an internal resolve, and that wealth of abilities that accompany fledging love. He seemed to have grown younger. His eyes acquired the flicker of youth, his limbs gained litheness. He felt life frolicking inside him. He was beginning to exude authentic charm.

Autumn with its golden leaves was already setting in. The *dachniki* were departing, and stillness and rain were setting in outside the windows.

Song resounded in the soul of Ivan Ivanovich as with one truly in love.

Nadenka would look at Ivan Ivanovich and be unable to tear herself away. She was drawn to him. She blushed upon meeting him, her eyes gazed trustingly.

At last, Nadenka left.

Kuku left, too.

CHAPTER THREE
KUKU AND KUKUREKU

The train plodded like a turtle toward Leningrad. The commuter cars jangled. Trina Rublis read a book. Her fingers, rubicund from the setting sun, turned the rose-shaded pages. She was absorbed in the plot and skipped over the descriptions. She would again have a man. She was at peace.

Svistonov stood by the window, fidgeted nervously.

They hired a carriage not far from the monument. An hour later, the Hotel Angleterre appeared.[1]

Svistonov helped Trina out of her coat, dimmed the light, sat down at the desk. The deaf girl went about remaking the bed. She took off the blanket, the sheets, then spread them out again. She beat the pillows. She was bored. It didn't seem like domestic bliss.

Svistonov worked. He wrote, read, and behaved as if at home. He was transferring living beings and, somewhat pitying them, doing his best to narcotize them with the rhythms and music of vowels and intonation.

There was, to be honest, nothing for him to write about. He simply would take someone and transfer him. Because he possessed talent, however, and because to him there was no principle difference between the living and the dead, and because he had his own world of ideas, everything turned out in a strange and unprecedented light. Musicality in art, politeness in life—these were Svistonov's shields. That is why he turned pale whenever he committed a tactless act.

The deaf girl, without having waited for Svistonov, slept. The electric lamp, despite the sunrise, glowed all the same. Pages were being covered with small, uneven handwriting. A notebook was taken out and consulted nervously, hastily. The hands of the man at work quivered like those of an alcoholic. He turned around to see if she had awaken, if she might interrupt him. But the deaf girl was sleeping, and a girlish expression had returned to her face. And this girlish expression distracted Svistonov from the world emerging in front of him. He lay aside his pencil, walked over to her on tip-toe, undressed, and sat at the bedside. He tenderly caressed the deaf girl's head, watched her closed mouth, listened to her even breathing. He felt safe. She would not overhear his thoughts, would not pass along to anybody the intricacies of his creativity. With her he could talk about whatever he felt like. This was the ideal listener. Let rumors fly, let them say whatever they wanted about him. He would not go so far as to live with her, though; he did not need her for that. He then began thinking that it wouldn't be right to neglect her altogether, that perhaps her figure, or her past, present, even future, might prove useful for one of his chapters. He began recalling everything he had heard about her. Sitting back down at the table, immersed in thought, he began transferring her, too, into literature. It was accompanied by symptoms of illness: heart palpitations, trembling hands, chills, and a tension headache that fatigued the whole body. By morning Svistonov was sitting like a dummy in front of the window. He felt like screaming from anguish. He felt a sickly desolation in his mind.

Come daytime they had coffee and parted. The deaf girl smiled crookedly. Svistonov headed off to work. He bought a newspaper, read through it, and grew vengeful. He despised any newspaper in which he was panned. He knew that later the reviewer, running into him on the publishing house stairs, would take him aside and begin apologizing.

"You know how it is. The time requires it. I liked your books very much, but you yourself understand, Andrey Nikolayevich. I had to pan you."

Indeed while Svistonov was climbing the stairs, the reviewer ran up to him.

"Do you know who you're dealing with!" Svistonov quavered. "Oh, how I'll disgrace you! You think you're just a small fry for me!"

After returning home, Svistonov tried all evening to exact his revenge on the reviewer, but he could not. The person was not of literary interest to him. Without wasting any more time, he decided to head over to the lecture at the Geographic Society in order to meet up with Pasha.

"Nadenka's a delightful girl, isn't she?" Svistonov asked during the intermission. "Kuku, so it seems, has fallen in love with her."

"He'll deceive her," said Pasha, reddening. "A person gifted with such knowledge is dangerous. I was at the Film Institute Ball yesterday, and Kuku danced with her all evening long. He didn't let me get close. He strutted around her like a rooster."

"I tell you what, Pasha. Let's forget about the lecture and go have a beer."

"Thanks, Andrey Nikolayevich. "I'd love something to drink."

"And don't you despair, Pasha, she'll come back to you."

"If I had the money, I'd drink myself into oblivion, Andrey Nikolayevich!"

"Take care of your talent," responded Svistonov. "Believe me, all of this is nonsense, my dear little Pasha. Save yourself for literature. Have you written a story about your life, as I advised you? It'll take your mind off your unhappy passion. And in the meantime Nadenka will come back to you."

Pasha took out his notebook.

"These are my confessions. Only promise, Andrey Nikolayevich, not to show anyone."

"I'll read it intently," said Svistonov, putting the manuscript in his pocket. "So tell me...did Kuku dance brilliantly? Yes, and was she glowing? And did Kuku...did he escort her home? Did they take a carriage? Did Kuku give the doorman a good tip? Let's see, you wanted something to drink...."

"Not once all evening did Nadenka call on me, Andrey Nikolayevich! And why weren't you there, Andrey Nikolayevich?"

"I forgot to come," Svistonov answered. "I tell you what, Pasha, today I received some money. Let's go out to the islands.[2] You'll have fun."

"I'd like to eat something spicy, Andrey Nikolayevich."

"That's right," said Svistonov, "herring and ice cream. A little something spicy with a little something cold has a way of relieving sorrow." And Svistonov, regretting that he had not been at the Film Institute, decided to take Pasha for a ride, just like Kuku had taken Nadenka for a ride from the Film Institute. "Would you like some flowers, Pasha?" Svistonov asked.

Pasha looked at him with surprise. They walked past the Bolshoy Drama Theater, past the Apraksin Market, past Gostinyy Dvor.

Svistonov bought Pasha flowers.

Through the deserted islands rode a carriage. Inside it were Svistonov and Pasha.

"All right?" inquired Svistonov.

"Very."

"What does this greenery remind you of, Pasha?"

Pasha, morosely:

I love nature's luxuriant fading,
Forests decked in crimson and gold. . . .[3]

"The answer is more for Kuku, not for Nadenka," thought Svistonov.

"Which orchestra played at the Film Institute?" During the entire ride, Svistonov reconstructed the evening at the Film Institute and conversed with Pasha in the same way, to his mind, that Kuku had spoken with Nadenka. Then, reclining, he took out his notebook and began writing.

Kukureku and Verochka exited the Bolshoy Drama Theater.

"Verochka," said Kukureku, "let's go out to the islands, where Blok used to ride around."

"Shall we go in an automobile?" asked Verochka.

"If you like," answered Kukureku. "Although I'd prefer a carriage."

"No, no, in an automobile!"

"In that case, let's head over to Gostinyy Dvor. Do you like flowers?" asked Kukureku. Upon crossing the street with Verochka, he bought three roses.

They walked past the empty arcades of Gostinyy Dvor, past the watchmen dozing behind the drawn ropes, and came out onto Prospect of the 25th of October.

"Do you like this street, Verochka?" Kukureku asked. "To think how many times it has been the subject of literary treatment. The beauty of it!"

Verochka walked along, her eyes opened wide, pressing the flowers to her chest. She was thinking that here her dream was being fulfilled, a beautiful life was commencing. She was slightly regretful, though, that the action wasn't unfolding in Berlin, where the asphalt shined so that it reflected all the automobiles and the people. Kukureku hired a taxicab, helped Verochka in, and off they rode to the islands.

Kukureku looked off to the sides…

But Pasha stirred.

"What are you writing, Andrey Nikolayevich?"

"One minute, Pasha." Svistonov hurried to finish the sketch.

Kukureku escorted Verochka up to the gate. The dawn was illuminating the upper floors of the buildings. He looked out onto the Aleksandrovskiy Garden and sighed:

> I love nature's luxuriant fading,
> Forests decked in crimson and gold....

Having uttered this verse, Kukureku kissed Verochka's hand and withdrew, whistling. He was satisfied that, like Blok, he had controlled himself and had delivered Verochka home safely.

After returning home and having a rest, Svistonov took up a book. He read slowly, as if he were strolling through an enchanting neighborhood. He loved to ponder each phrase, to sit a while, to smoke. Passages that intrigued him most he reread in both old and new translations. The night passed imperceptibly. He turned to thoughts of the coming day, what to undertake, where to go. Watching the tram racing by, the people hurrying along, the yellow piles of sand, he began writing a letter to a friend of his requesting to have placed at his disposal candy wrappers, written notes, and diaries of relatives and acquaintances, promising to return everything safe and intact.

Then he decided to get some sleep. As he was lying down, it seemed to him that he knew to the last detail not only the words and the comings and goings of Ivan Ivanovich, but also the man's innermost thoughts. Now he could get down to his systematic creativity. He concluded that the overall picture of

Kuku must in no way be tampered with, that Kuku's side-whiskers were indispensable, that his passion for Detskoye Selo as well must be left alone, that anything better than in life itself was not possible to conceive. Perhaps once everything was written, it might be possible to change a thing or two, but for now even the choice of surname had to be left along the same lines. Not Kuku, but Kukureku, the name quickly thought up during the nighttime ride.

Ivan Ivanovich manifested on paper. Here and there the self-satisfied figure began to pop up on the pages: here he enjoyed himself sitting on a divan once having belonged to Dostoyevskiy; there, at the Pushkin House, he read books from Pushkin's library; here again, he strolled around Yasnaya Polyana.[4] The building in which Kuku lived was deployed as well—Svistonov, admittedly, moved the building to another part of the city—and the way Kuku spoke was portrayed.

Svistonov treated even himself unceremoniously. He took any of the objects standing on the nearby table or a fact from his own biography and attached it to someone. And later everyone gasps, "Look how he scandalizes himself!" and rumors fly, one more astounding than the next. And Svistonov himself exacerbates the gossip.

He brought the half-finished portrait of Kuku, rolled up like a tube, to the company of still rather young *spletniki*, literary enthusiasts eager for scandal.[5]

The company had been awaiting Svistonov's arrival, preparing themselves to be filled with admiration, to delight in the correlation between the contrived and the real, to rouse themselves, to feed their minds and imaginations.

"Oh, that Svistonov!" they would say. "How amusingly he writes! And who is Kamadasheva? It's probably Anna Petrovna Ramadasheva."

The collective of *spletniki* considered themselves true connoisseurs of literature. They would latch onto a writer of any kind and ask of him to deliver pleasure.

And the writer, presuming that he is reading to people in all innocence, goes ahead and reads. And the eyes of one of the listening young men shine and his whole being blossoms. Then he pats the writer playfully on the shoulder and says, "I could tell—Kamadasheva, without doubt, is Ramadasheva. Say, the construction of your work is similar to the construction of Pavel Nikolayevich's." The writer, stunned, sits down. "What a stupid mistake," he muses. "Why the hell did I read to them?"

The city's *spletniki* were broken down into circles. Members of each circle were acquainted with one another. When the rumor had circulated that Svistonov was planning to hold a reading at Nadezhda Semyonovna's, her *spletniki* began waiting for an invitation. Several even visited Nadezhda Semyonovna beforehand to find out if they could bring their acquaintances from another circle.

When Svistonov arrived he thus found an assemblage in full bloom. On divans, poufs, chairs, the floor, and the windowsills sat the young, the mature, the elderly. All were waiting for him and conversing boisterously.

Svistonov kissed the hand of every *spletnitsa,* shook the hand of every *spletnik,* and settled in comfortably at a small table. Nadezhda Semyonovna, the hostess, sat closer than the rest so as not to miss a single word. Everyone listened attentively.

From time to time arose a snigger or an exchange of whispers. They recognized some of their acquaintances, couldn't recognize several others. They asked each other in the ear, "Who is that?" and their faces grew distressed. And finally, like lightening, a conjecture flashed, and they again took to whispering. At the conclusion of the reading, they thronged around Svistonov and voiced their admiration.

"No, no," Svistonov said in such a way that everyone sensed, "Yes, yes."

They all sat down at a table for tea. The samovar gurgled, pastries crunched. It was at this time that Svistonov started collecting new bits of gossip.

"Say, have you heard what happened? Aleksey Ivanovich has taken a new lease on life. Married a complete youngster. Now there's a good main character for you!...

"What material, I tell you. You could just die. And how peculiarly he married her. He went out specially to Detskoye Selo, closer to the penates of Pushkin, and had the ceremony there in the Cathedral of St. Sofia."

"For Kukureku," thought Svistonov, "precisely for Kukureku."

"And then there's Nikandrov. His whole life he's been looking for a girl straight out of Turgyenev. He hit forty and finally found one. And he married her. Now he's living in bliss too!"

Svistonov left. The gossip shot around the city: Kukureku was none other than Kuku! And so Svistonov encroached on what might be called *Intimität des Mensches*, publicly laid Kuku bare, and what's more, portrayed him in such a manner as to declass Kuku. Svistonov had long since forgotten about his conversation with the deaf girl, provoked, as it was, by momentary irritability.

Arriving home with fresh impressions, Svistonov began augmenting one of his chapters.

Gradually Kukureku was convinced that Verochka was a girl out of a Turgyenev novel, that in her there was something of Liza. He felt his love all the more strongly. His soul trembled. Verochka's mother allowed her to go out with Kukureku, and together they visited the Pushkin House, the Literary Bridges Cemetery, and even rode out to Mikhaylovskoye Selo.[6] *Their romance flowed tranquilly. Kukureku often listened to Verochka play the piano. Sitting in an easy chair, he sometimes felt like Lavretskiy. All the more tenderly Verochka played Chopin, and darker and darker the room became, and finally the electric candles flared.*

In reality, Kuku was falling deeper and deeper in love with Nadenka. For lack of time, he met with Svistonov all the more infrequently and still did not know that Svistonov had already lived his life for him. Kuku and Nadenka had been going out to the environs of the city. They, too, visited Mikhaylovskoye Selo. Only Kuku did not compare Nadenka to Liza, but to Natasha. And he believed that she would forever remain Natasha and not a mere woman.

The gossip spread. Kuku was spied on to see how he was walking down a path already written. Finally, the gossip reached Kuku. He fell into rapture. At long last, he had made it into literature.

He informed Nadenka about it as if it were the grandest event of his life.

"Nadenka," he said importantly, taking her by the hand, "I am in such rapture. Our friend Svistonov has immortalized me! He has written a novel about me. From what I hear, it's wonderful. They're saying that not since the Symbolists has such a novel appeared, that it's written in an exceptional style, and that it captures our entire epoch."

"But weren't you going to be writing together?"

"I'm lazy, Nadenka, nothing came of it."

Nadenka gazed at Ivan Ivanovich. She respected him, considered him a most intelligent person.

"Well, then, fine, Ivan Ivanovich," she said affectionately. "I am so, so happy you are pleased. Andrey Nikolayevich often told me that he likes you very much, that you are an exceptionally interesting person."

"I feel like it's my name-day in some way. Nadenka, let's go to the Neva and take a walk. Let's go. We'll buy a cake and celebrate this event....

"My sweet Nadenka," Kuku continued, "soon, soon we shall celebrate our wedding. It will be just your friends and my friends. But in the meantime, don't tell anybody. We shall send out cards. 'So-and-so and so-and-so request the honor of your presence in Detskoye Selo at the Cathedral of St. Sofia....'"

A letter from Lenochka, staying in the town of Staraya Russa, to Svistonov:

My Sunshine,

How is your new novel coming along? Are you having to work hard on it? Don't tire yourself out. Sleep at night and eat properly.

How is your Pole, Count, and Georgian? Did you get hold of the necessary material? I read in the newspapers that your novel will be appearing soon.

You asked me to write what I remember about Liza from A Nest of the Gentry. *How lazy you are, my precious! I'm only teasing, Andryushenka! I've understood that you need to know what sticks in the memory about her manner. After dinner I led a discussion. I write to you in the participants' words:*

Older woman, thin, 48 years old, long-nosed:

Liza loved to be alone, to read the Holy Scripture. She loved nature, birds. Loved to dream. She had no girlfriends. In childhood her nanny had a great influence on her. She considered it a sin that she fell in love with Lavretskiy, a married man, considered herself guilty.

School teacher, 26 years old:

Daughter of a landowner. A very vague image. A garden. She's leaving for a convent because she has fallen in love with Lavretskiy. Instead of fairy tales, her nanny used to read her biographies of holy martyrs. She would wake her up early and take her to church.

Local critic:

I remember absolutely nothing. I read it so long ago that nothing remains.

Local Don Juan:

I remember Lavretskiy standing on the stairs. The sun is shining through Liza's hair. I remember her taking a walk with the old man. I remember the postcards. He is sitting, she is standing with a fishing pole.

That is all that I could gather for you today, Andryushenka. Just imagine what a bore it is here. They talk only about their illnesses and how much money their husbands make. Kisses.

Seated against a background of books long since opened, Svistonov began writing the next chapter. The work went well, the atmosphere was well-suited. Svistonov loved flowers, and violets stood in a large cut-glass tumbler on the table.

Svistonov wrote in the past tense, sometimes in the very past. It was as if that which he described had long ago come to an end, as if he were using not pulsating reality but phenomena long dead. He wrote about his own epoch as another writer might write about distant times not entirely familiar to the reader. He generalized events of everyday life instead of individualizing them. Unwittingly, he described the present using a historical method that was extraordinarily insulting to his contemporaries.

The writing came to Svistonov like the writing had never come before. An entire city emerged before him, and in this imaginary city his characters moved about, drank, conversed, and married. Svistonov felt himself in a state of emptiness—or better yet, in a theater, in a dim loge, sitting in the role of a young, elegant, romantically spirited spectator. At this moment he loved his characters to the utmost. They seemed enlightened to him. Both the rhythm he felt inside and his insatiable desire for harmony had affected the choice and the order of the words lying on the page.

There was a knock at the door; the enchantment faded. "Who could that be?" Svistonov wondered irritably. "I probably shouldn't answer. Always being interrupted." He listened.

The knock came again. "What the hell!" Svistonov whispered. "I'm not even allowed to get a little work done. All the same, I won't be able to write anymore." After closing his folder, he unlocked the door. On the porch stood Kuku.

"Forgive me, Andrey Nikolayevich," Kuku uttered, "for bursting in on you so unexpectedly. But you know how it is, things to do. Prenuptial delirium!"

"Please, come in," replied Svistonov and helped Kuku out of his coat.

"Well, what's new with you?" Kuku asked. "How's the writing going? I hear that your novel is coming along splendidly."

Svistonov fussed with the manuscript.

"Still far from finished," he replied.

"And might just a little excerpt be permissible? They say I'm already in it."

"Ivan Ivanovich, come now. For pity's sake!" Svistonov replied.

"But I've been hearing that I—" and Kuku, self-important and portly, became stricken with grief. "Why, of course not, Andrey Nikolayevich. After all, it couldn't be." He stopped, then said: "For the sake of old friendship, read some."

Svistonov decided it poor-spirited to refuse. He seated himself in his multi-colored armchair, took the manuscript, and commenced reading his novel.

As the reading went on, Kuku's face took on an expression of admiration and astonishment.

"What style!" he shook his head. "What profundity! Andrey Nikolayevich, I wouldn't have thought you would reveal yourself so."

Svistonov continued reading. By now Kukureku had appeared, and Kuku had turned pale. He sunk down into his chair and listened to the end, his mouth open.

"Andrey Nikolayevich, why, it's..."

After the reading, Ivan Ivanovich went outside, pale. He saw himself now totally exposed and unprotected, at odds with a world laughing at him. Fear was on Ivan Ivanovich's face, and across it straggled an awkward, apologetic smile. Singed and dejected by his own image, he was afraid of running into anybody he knew. He felt that everyone could see clearly his worthlessness, that no one would bow to him, that they would all turn away and walk past him, intentionally conversing on gaily with their companion, wife, girlfriend. Tears appeared in Ivan Ivanovich's eyes. Racked with lament for himself, he stopped and saw Svistonov heading off somewhere.

In the evening Kuku did not leave his enormous building as usual, did not drop in on Nadenka to take a walk with her and spend a little of the evening together, but rather he locked himself in his room. He did not know what to do. He was of a mind to kill Svistonov, who had taken his life away.

Practically in tears, he envisioned himself smashing one side of Svistonov's face and then the other, punching out all his teeth, poking out his eyes, and dragging the body through the streets. But Kuku remembered that he, Kuku, was a cultured person and that this was not possible. He wept and decided to write a letter. But he remembered that Kukureku had already written such a letter for him. Suddenly the thought of Nadenka cut through his heart. He imagined her reading Svistonov's novel. He saw her carried away by the rhythm, beginning to smirk at her betrothed, beginning to laugh and despise him.

In the next room, a voice was singing the aria of the nanny from *Yevgeniy Onegin*. Kuku banged on the wall with his fists, and all grew quiet. A dreadful silence set in, then steps and a voice were heard, "Don't interrupt people practicing!" Kuku, respectable and rotund, sat at his desk and mused that another person had already lived his life for him, had lived it pitifully and despicably, that now there was nothing for him, Kuku, to do, that now he himself was no longer interested in Nadenka, that he no longer loved her and could not marry her, that it would be a redundancy, an insufferable passing of one and the same life, that even if Svistonov indeed tore up his manuscript, nonetheless he, Kuku, his whole life would know that the self-respect inside him had been irreversibly destroyed, that life had lost for him all its appeal.

In the morning, Kuku nevertheless went to see Svistonov. He had decided to hide from his friends and to tearfully implore Svistonov to tear up the manuscript.

"What, shall I kneel before you!" screamed Kuku. "If you are an honorable man, then you will rip up the manuscript! To mock a person respected by all! If we were living in a different time, there would be no escaping my seconds for you! But now," he whispered, covering his face with his hands, "the devil only knows...." Svistonov felt that before him no longer stood a person but something like a corpse.

"I implore you, Andrey Nikolayevich, give it to me, I'll destroy your manuscript...."

"Ivan Ivanovich," replied Svistonov, "why, it's not you I have depicted, not your soul. After all, it's not possible to depict a soul. True, I took a few details—"

But Kuku did not allow Svistonov to finish. He rushed over to the table, where the manuscript was lying. Svistonov, afraid that his world would be destroyed and wishing to distract Kuku, inquired:

"How is Nadezhda Nikolayevna getting along?"

A maddened face with clenched fists came up to Svistonov.

"You are not a man, you are but half a man! You are a vile creature! You know better than I what's going on with Nadezhda Nikolayevna!"

With clenched fists Kuku crossed the room.

The room had grown stuffy. Svistonov threw open the window and noticed that in the courtyard people were already returning from work, conversing. "I'm late," he thought, "I'll have to take it over to the typist tomorrow." Kuku was not leaving. He was sitting in the chair weighing things over.

Svistonov reflected that probably a few of the episodes

that so disturbed Kuku could be changed, that in the past he had indeed been accosted, but never had there been this kind of anguish.

Svistonov knew that not all his characters could turn out like Grammonts, that people would not be completely enraptured with their portrayals, as the marshal's brother was upon seeing himself portrayed in Molière's *Le Mariage forcé*. Nevertheless, he had not imagined that it would tell on Kuku so strongly.

"It's time for me to go," said Svistonov, grimacing and standing up as Kuku dressed.

They left together. Svistonov held the manuscript. Kuku glanced at the manuscript and was silent. He struggled with the desire to snatch the manuscript and run off. Without saying a word to one another, they parted at a crossroads.

Kuku did not come, did not write. Trying days set in for Nadenka. She would enter his city-like building but would not find Ivan Ivanovich in. No longer was he around, high-spirited and respectable, to proffer his hand to her upon meeting. His bass voice no longer resounded. Occasionally from the courtyard she would see a light in his window and go up to his apartment only to ring the bell in vain.

Ivan Ivanovich had descended into a living hell. The image of Kukureku stood before him in all its absurdity and stupidity. Ivan Ivanovich no longer went out to the city environs. He shaved his side-whiskers, changed his attire, and moved to a different part of the city. There Ivan Ivanovich nonetheless felt utterly wretched, felt that he had become, literally, only half a man, that everything inside him had been stolen. What remained in him and around him was only filth, embitterment, suspicion, self-doubt.

He changed physically. He became thinner, his lips pursed, his countenance took on an embittered, disgusted expression.

Having become half a man, Ivan Ivanovich began to seek a new destiny.

Of the opinion that Svistonov mocked respect for great individuals in general, Kuku began to despise great individuals. Now he would tell an old acquaintance that it was wrong not only to sit complacently on Dostoyevskiy's couch but even to keep couches of Dostoyevskiy, relics of Pushkin, and the like, that all of it should be burned for seeding pernicious thoughts and provoking pernicious desires.

He took Svistonov's laughter at the fanfare of love for laughter at love in general and began saying that there was no such thing as love, that there is only contiguity of epiderms.

Afraid of running into his old acquaintances, he decided to move to a different city.

Svistonov, having committed spiritual manslaughter, was at peace.

"It happened according to given laws," he thought. "Kuku was not a genuine person. I acted immorally, taking advantage of him for my novel. In any case, he shouldn't have read it before the finishing touches were applied, before he appeared as a type. He believed in me, in my friendship. My act was unethical, but Kuku unexpectedly showed up at my apartment, I had no way out. It was, all and all, involuntary manslaughter.

CHAPTER FOUR
THE SOVIET CAGLIOSTRO

Psikhachyov lived on the embankment of the Big Neva River in a modest-sized, wooden house, from which he traveled to all parts of Russia. The house was quiet and amazingly transparent.[1] In front of it was a quiet little garden and the quiet embankment, barren of people.

In the distance was a cafe and a small cooperative with dirty windows.

No one knew that here lived the Soviet Cagliostro.

Flowers in little yellow pots stood on the window sills. The self-proclaimed doctor of philosophy was strolling through the garden thinking over his plan for a new venture, a hypnosis seance in the town of Volkhov.

Everybody knows of Volkhov, where the houses stand as if on hens' legs, where a factory club manager will organize a dance in the club on the name-day of his wife, where sleight of hand artists arrive once every couple of years.[2] Volkhov has never seen real artists.

The good-natured cynic was strolling through the garden and thinking things over. In his daughter's room, beneath a pink lampshade with a floral design, a light bulb still burned. The father went over to the window and peered in. "Sweet child," he thought, "going to bed. She doesn't know how hard it is for her father to put food on the table."

The Soviet Cagliostro was sad on this evening.

A lone passerby hurried along the embankment.

The passerby struck a match and held it to a piece of paper taken from his pocket.

Psikhachyov recognized Svistonov and went out through the gate.

"Looking for me?" he asked.

"No, not for you," replied Svistonov. "I'll drop in on you tomorrow. Today I'm off to another house."

"You're lying," Psikhachyov muttered, waving his hand.

"But my, how it stinks in here," said Svistonov, entering the room the following day and looking around. "You really never change into comfortable clothes or even take off your shoes? You sleep on that couch? What a monstrous blanket you've got! I'm so worn out already today, dear Vladimir Yevgenyevich!"

From the table Svistonov picked up a small picture.

"Is this you as a baby?"

"Make yourself at home. Look around."

"And you'll allow me to take a look through your correspondences? Letters to you, letters from you—it's all extremely interesting. May I open it?" asked Svistonov, walking over to the dresser.

"So, a tail-coat, moth-eaten… and there must be a top hat. Have you kept one? And where is your family album?" inquired Svistonov.

The host withdrew and brought back an album with a lacquered cover. His guest went through the pages, examined picture postcards, dreamt. Psikhachyov stood by the table, his fists propping up his head.

"Introduce me to your family," said Svistonov.

"No, by no means…" Vladimir Yevgenyevich began to redden.

His fourteen year-old daughter came running in.

"Papa, Papa, the countess is asking for you."

"Just a minute, Masha." Psikhachyov bustled about and slipped behind the door.

Svistonov approached the teenager.

"Let's get acquainted," he said.

Masha curtsied.

"You must be studying in middle school, am I right?" asked Svistonov, letting go of her hand.

"No, Papa doesn't let me."

Svistonov noted her frail and smartly dressed little figure. Psikhachyov ran in.

"Out, out, Masha!"

The daughter glanced at Svistonov coquettishly.

"Out, I said!"

Masha left. In a minute she came running in again.

"Papa, the prince has arrived."

"For God's sake, forgive me." Taking Masha by the hand, Psikhachyov again slipped behind the door. The portière was drawn shut. Svistonov smoked and waited. He allowed his gaze to wander over the spines of Psikhachyov's dusty, moldy books and began to read their titles.

"What's with all the nobility calling on you?"

"Pure chance," replied Psikhachyov, embarrassed.

"Well, fine. What is it then you intend to tell me?"

"Does it interest you—who is living with whom?"

"To tell you the truth, very little."

"What then interests you?"

"Your observations of the last several years. Your feelings and thoughts. Tell me, why did you strive to denounce science?"

"I considered it original."

"You, of course, in your youth wrote poetry?"

"About the clap."

"Cheerful!"

"Very cheerful."

A voice rang out from behind the door.

"Papa, Papa, Mama's calling."

"Just a minute, little one."

Svistonov walked over to the bookshelf. He opened a book by Blok to a bookmarked page.

No longer dreams of tenderness and fame,
All that has ended, youth as well has gone!

Svistonov stifled his laughter. He walked over to the window.

Downstairs, Psikhachyov was returning from the cooperative with a roll.

In Psikhachyov's living room was a small library of books on the occult, freemasonry, magic. But Svistonov gathered that Psikhachyov did not believe in the occult, freemasonry, or magic.

Everybody loves examining things. Girls and women like dreaming over fashion magazines; an engineer, being jarred by a representation of foreign engine; a little old man, crying over a photograph of his deceased children.

Psikhachyov, his head swaying from side to side, leafed through pictures of mandrakes resembling old men, talismans engraved with Sun, Moon, and Mars, geomantic trees, tables of sephiroths, images of demons, the stocky Azazel leading a goat, the Mephistopheles-like Haborim flying on a serpent, the winged, slightly bony Ashtaroth with gaping eyes.

In his youth, Psikhachyov wanted to be a seducer. From 1908 to 1912 he indeed dressed in white and wore a black velvet cap with a red feather. Relatives considered it a rich man's whimsy.

As a young man, Psikhachyov spent pleasant nights behind treatises concerning the proper way to enter into pacts with spirits. Dreamy nights.

Among common folk he had the reputation of a mystic. Psikhachyov in his early years enjoyed this tremendously. Even now he liked it when he was regarded timorously. There were rumors about him, that he was a hierophant of some kind of secret order, that he had ascended through the ranks and reached the top. He claimed that he was a Thessalonian Greek by birth, and Thessalonica, as is well known, was famous for its sorcery.

In one of the little rooms of his house were portraits from the times of Catherine and Aleksandr as well as of Greek men and women in wigs and caftans, a mother-of-pearl crucifix standing inside a bell jar meant for a clock, a 1930s family album containing watercolors, verses, vignettes, and a Greek bible bearing the surnames Rali, Hari, Marazli.

Svistonov, having surveyed the apartment, fell in love with the Soviet Cagliostro. "How sad is his life!" he thought. "What does his repute as the Soviet Cagliostro give him when he himself knows he's a pretender, that he's not at all a Greek nor a soothsayer but simply Vladimir Yevgenyevich Psikhachyov. Let even the Pope in Rome send him his blessing every year. For after all, he doesn't even believe in the Pope."

Seated in the bedroom beneath antique portraits, the host and guest smoked and drank a little vodka chased with tomatoes.

Psikhachyov spoke of his order. Svistonov enjoyed his cigarette, inhaling and letting the smoke out his nostrils. He was seeing Psikhachyov's night, for in the life of every man there is a great night of doubt followed by either victory or defeat. A night which may last months and years.

To the sound of Psikhachyov's speech Svistonov tried to summon back the actual night at hand.

When Psikhachyov was young, even the leaves sounded differently and even the birds sung differently. He had believed that he would be able to rip off the world's glossy coating, that he was something like a devil. He had ridden like the wind atop a black stallion leading a cavalcade. The youths had regaled themselves on candy as they urged on their steeds, joking merrily.

Svistonov's heart sank.

In all seriousness, there should be no discounting the works and days of Svistonov. His life consisted of not only listening to conversations and hunting for people but also of a peculiar infection by his subjects, a certain spiritual complicity in their lives. That is why when his characters died, something died inside Svistonov as well; when they repudiated something, Svistonov too experienced a certain share of repudiation. Moreover, as odd as it may seem, Svistonov truly believed in the magical power of the word.

Psikhachyov, noticing that Svistonov had turned pale, assumed that he had produced a strong impression on his guest.

"Psikhachyov-Rali-Hari-Marazli!" Svistonov sarcastically broke the silence. "Tell me, how did you enter into a pact with the devil? You're a very interesting man, I'll gladly use you in my novel," continued Svistonov.

The owner of the quiet apartment was utterly heartened. Sweet, celebratory, delightful music resounded around him and little by little grew louder and louder such that it seemed the harmonious sounds of it were filling the entire room, spilling out the window into the small front garden and reaching the walls of the neighboring house. The kind of music heard by a bride and bridegroom if they are extremely young and very much in love.

Psikhachyov got up from the couch, straightened himself.

"In order to enter into a pact with one of the main spirits, I went out, and with a new knife, never used before, cut off a sprig from a wild nut tree, inscribed a triangle in a remote area, set down two candles, stood in the middle of the triangle, and pronounced the great invocation, 'Emperor Lucifer, god of all rebellious spirits, be favorable to my call...."'

Svistonov smiled.

"Vladimir Yevgenyevich, I'm not asking you about that kind of pact, but about the pact within you."

"That is, what?"

"About the moment when you could feel that you'd lost your will, when you acknowledged that you're ruined, that you're a pretender."

The music stopped. In front of Psikhachyov sat a man drinking vodka and making fun of him. Everything suddenly became repugnant to him somehow, and he even seemed to himself some kind of uninteresting creature. After a minute, he grew agitated.

"How is that again—I'm a pretender?" he asked. "In other words, you don't believe that I'm a doctor of philosophy?" The host's face grew malicious and spiteful.

"Why, no," answered the guest politely. "I'm referring to something completely different. You call yourself a mystic, but maybe you're not a mystic at all. You say, 'I am an idealist,' but maybe you're not an idealist at all."

Vladimir Yevgenyevich grimaced.

"Or maybe by repeating to one and all, albeit with a grin, that you're a mystic, you believe that you actually will become one? It's for my novel," continued the guest, smiling. "Don't be angry. I have to test you, you know. Why, I'm only joking about the whole thing."

Psikhachyov's face brightened and his eyes beamed.

Svistonov stared at this man speaking about gymnosophists, Isis's priests, the Eleusinian Mysteries, and the Pythagorean School, evidently without much knowledge of any of it. In any case, with less knowledge than he might have had.

"Is everything all right?" asked the host. "Do you like it here?"

"Very much," answered Svistonov. "Here one sits right beside a devotee…." Svistonov's voice became dreamy.

Psikhachyov did his best to speak in such a way that it would be perfectly clear to Svistonov that the speaker belonged to a powerful and secret society.

The host, all and all, was a sweet man. He called May "adarmapagon"; June, "hardat"; July, "terma"; August, "med-erme"; and his house, "Eleusis."[3] At times he even signed his own surname numerically, thus:

15, 18, 4, 10, 5, 12, 19, 10, 5, 8, 7, 7.

And he flourished the signature.

True, it came out somewhat long; but then again, instead of "psikha" he got "Psisha."[4] On more secretive documents, he wrote in special hieroglyphs and called himself Mephistopheles.

There is no need for the reader to know what the host and his guest discussed that evening; it is necessary to know only that they warmly exchanged kisses on the threshold, the guest disappeared into the darkness of night, and the host for some time watched him exaltedly before heading upstairs with a candle.

All night Psikhachyov did not sleep, his shadow moving from corner to corner in his room. He was mulling something over. Then he sat at his desk and began covering a piece of paper with numerals.

Svistonov walked through the fog wondering about what might happen if both of them believed in the existence of evil powers.

At the appointed time in the evening, as late as possible, the novice Svistonov was admitted into a faintly lit room. Psikhachyov's voice carried out from behind a curtain. On a large table in the middle of the room lay a naked sword. A large, cut glass icon-lamp bathed the entire scene in gentle light.

From behind the curtain Psikhachyov's voice asked Svistonov:

"Do you persist in your wish—to be admitted?"

After Svistonov's affirmative reply, Psikhachyov's voice directed the new applicant to a dark room for meditation.

Summoned back, Svistonov beheld Psikhachyov at the table with the sword in his hand. Questions followed questions. Finally, it came:

"Your wish is just. In the name of the supremely blessed order from which I receive my power and my strength, and in the name of all its members, I promise you protection, justice, and support."

Here Psikhachyov raised the sword—Svistonov noticed that the sword was not very old—and pressed the tip of the blade against Svistonov's chest. With pathos he continued:

"But if you should become a traitor, if you should make of yourself a perjurer, then know..."

After laying the sword on the table, Psikhachyov commenced reading a blessing, which Svistonov repeated after him. Then Svistonov pronounced the oath.

"Congratulations," said Psikhachyov.

They went downstairs and set off for a cafe.

Psikhachyov led Svistonov smoothly by the arm to meet his society. They were all women, not so young anymore. Svistonov's nostrils were tickled unpleasantly by the odor of their perfumes. Their unnatural, languid movements wore unpleasantly on Svistonov's eyes. Several of them smoked perfumed cigarettes; others discussed elevated things such as whether or not tables can fly.

Brought in by Psikhachyov as a stranger to these strange women, Svistonov made a general bow and stood upright. The hostess approached Svistonov and said:

"You are a friend of Psikhachyov, therefore you are a friend of ours."

Svistonov smiled obligingly.

"Allow me to introduce you." Psikhachyov, taking the initiative, went from one lady to another introducing Svistonov.

They reminded Svistonov of animals. One was a little goat, another, a little horse, a third, a little dog. He experienced a sensation of insurmountable antipathy, yet his face expressed a deferential tenderness.

"You are a man of belles-lettres, Andrey Nikolayevich?

We love all the arts beyond expression. Vladimir Yevgenyevich recently was telling us about you."

Svistonov could only bow.

So as to avoid a silence and to allow the guest a chance to relax, the hostess went over to Psikhachyov and asked him to keep his promise by playing each member her leitmotif.

Psikhachyov assented.

Svistonov studied the hostess. He read in her an egoism, skillful and polite, which characterizes people under the influence of Mercury, as Psikhachyov had said, people who know how to make their faults serve their interests. She was steadfast and sly.

Psikhachyov played her the appropriate piece.

"There is no doubt," observed Svistonov silently, "that Psikhachyov does possess a gift for improvisation, has a wonderful memory, knows the old masters, can counterpoint unexpectedly bizarre themes, and can surprise."

Psikhachyov played each lady her leitmotif in turn. The listeners sat motionless in delight. Psikhachyov glanced triumphantly at Svistonov.

"I was playing for you," he said in a whisper. "Specially for you!"

Svistonov clasped him by the elbow.

"Today we are like the hypostasis of Orpheus. You are the words, I am the music," beamed Psikhachyov.

"Yes," confirmed Svistonov with feigned enthusiasm.

In the company of the ladies, Psikhachyov felt devastating.

"Our silence has conveyed more to you than applause would have." The hostess moved over to the men standing by the piano.

A general conversation about music and souls arose.

The conversation shifted to Psikhachyov's recent tenure in Italy. Psikhachyov took out a statuette of a three-faced Hekate and began showing it all around.

"The little nose it's got," he said. "Look here, it's round, and God only knows if it's real. I bought it in Naples. Now it goes with me everywhere." He put it back in his breast pocket. "Closer to the heart," he said and glanced at Svistonov sweetly.

"Shall I tell you about Isis?" he asked, taking a seat closer to the ladies, who were seated in a half-circle.

"Quite fascinating, please do!"

"Isis is a hermetic deity. Long hair flows down in waves to her divine neck. On top of her head is a disc, shiny like a mirror, sometimes between two coiled snakes.

Psikhachyov demonstrated how the snakes coil.

"She holds a sistrum in her right hand. On her left hangs a golden vessel. And the breath of this goddess is more aromatic than Arabian fragrances. I know all this from experience."

Psikhachyov did his best to affect an enigmatic expression with his eyes. He stood up from his chair, his arms rising in a ritualistic gesture.

"She is nature, the mother of all things, the goddess of the elements, the beginning of time, the tsarina of souls." Psikhachyov grew pale. "In the mysterious silence of the dark night, you will move us and set into motion objects without souls as well. I have accepted that fate is full of my long and difficult sufferings!

"Yes, you are approaching me quietly, a transparent apparition, in your ever-changing attire. Yes, I see the full moon and the stars and the flowers and the fruit!"

Psikhachyov fell silent.

Suddenly, from the corner of the room came a woman's squeaky voice:

"I am touched by your entreaty, Psikhachyov. I am the primordial mother of nature, the goddess of the elements...."

All heads turned around. It was Svistonov speaking.

But Psikhachyov recovered.

"You have driven away the apparition," he said.

The night passed unremarkably. Psikhachyov determined the colors of the ladies' souls. The soul of Marya Dmitriyevna turned out to be sky blue; Nadezhda Ivanovna's, pink; Yekaterina Borisovna's, pink turning lilac; and the hostess's, silver with black dots.

"Well, that's how we spend our time," said Psikhachyov, bidding farewell to Svistonov on the embankment in the morning rays of sunshine. "What do you think, pretty good?"

"Stupendous!" Svistonov replied. "Absolutely fantastic!"

Meanwhile a shop clerk named Yablochkin, whom Psikhachyov called Cato, was compiling his self-portrait at Psikhachyov's behest.

He wrote down the names and occupations of his parents and grandparents, listed his enemies, friends, and income, and searched his soul.

With fervor the new Cato took to reading Plutarch's Cato, delivered to him by the pretender hierophant. Questions rose before Yablochkin everywhere, and in the margins of the book he wrote question marks.

He lived on the sixth floor, the city lay beneath his feet. Dawn and daybreak lit up his room. He woke up earlier, went to bed later, and with every sunrise felt smarter and smarter.

Svistonov first met Cato at Psikhachyov's place. Seated beneath the antique portraits, the hierophant was explaining to his disciple the numerical alphabet.

Svistonov sat in another armchair with a collection of wonderful and memorable short stories and copied out on a piece of paper the page he needed:

La nuit de ce jour venue, le sorcier mena son compagnon par certaines montagnes et vallées, qu'il n'avaient que vus, et lui sembla qu'en peu de temps, ils avaient fait beaucoup de chemin. Puis entrant dans un champ tout enuironné de montagnes, il vit grand nombre d'hommes et de femmes qui s'amassaient lá, et vinrent tous à lui, menant grande fête…

Svistonov began speculating about what will happen to all these women and men after they read his book. Now they gleefully came out to meet him with pomp and circumstance, but later there could be a troubled din of opinions, wounded pride, betrayed friendships, ridiculed dreams.

Yablochkin was writing:

> 12, 11, 10, 9, 8, 7, 6,
> A, B, C, D, E, F, G.

Svistonov sat by the window like a shadow.

Psikhachyov believed in looking after his health. Strewn about were jars, glasses, and cups of sour milk, blackened by flies, and on the cracked windowsill lay ripening tomatoes.

"Your heart must be pure," Psikhachyov told Yablochkin, "and your spirit must burn with divine fire. The step you are taking is a most important one in your life. Promoting you to a knight of the order, we expect from you great and noble deeds worthy of the title."

Yablochkin felt he had communicated in a sacred rite. Upon leaving, he saw the world from another side. The city was ablaze with a different light somehow. People appeared before him in a new way, and he felt the need to apply himself to self-betterment and the enlightenment of others.

Svistonov guessed what was going on inside Yablochkin and felt bad about crushing the young man's dream, hauling him back to an aimless existence, exposing his consciousness to the Psikhachyov figure. He knew that Yablochkin would not fail to read his book, a book written by Psikhachyov's closest friend.

"Oh well, what will be will be. Psikhachyov is essential for my novel," decided Svistonov. Making himself more comfortable in Psikhachyov's room, in Psikhachyov's armchair, he began transferring Psikhachyov into the book.

The host was wiping off his relics. He was speaking about Yablochkin, formulating plans. The Neva was freezing up; soon Red Army soldiers would be advancing over it on skis. Soon a skating rink would be erected, and young people would dance inside the fenced space to the sounds of waltzes.

Svistonov regarded Psikhachyov. "Poor soul," he thought, "he asked for it himself."

"Say old fellow," he said, "how about heating the kettle, it's getting cold."

"Shall I light the stove?" asked the host.

"That would be just grand," answered the guest. "How splendidly we'll pass the time. Let there be snow outside the window. We'll sit here warm and snug."

Psikhachyov went out to the garden and brought back firewood.

Svistonov had written down everything he needed.

"Now, how about a game of cards," he said. He walked over to the stove and congenially rubbed his hands near the blazing fire, fell to thinking, then continued: "You must have cards, right? Let's set up the card table and ask your wife and daughter in to play whist."

Until midnight Svistonov played whist and lost. He enjoyed doing little favors. He noticed that Mrs. Psikhachyov's cheeks had flushed, and he read her thoughts about tomorrow's dinner, for which now it would be possible to buy the Burgundy her husband so loved. She would unfailingly invite this sweet Andrey Nikolayevich, whose friendship had so enlivened her husband.

Psikhachyov handled the chalk deftly. He had grown red as well.

They took turns shuffling the cards. The cards were tattered, greasy, with gold edges. They were so worn they may as well have been marked.

Svistonov was losing. He was content. He was able to pay

his hosts at least something for the hospitality.

Snow fell outside the windows with splendid little thuds. Above the players' heads hung splendid portraits. Masha and Svistonov sat with their backs to the darkened window. Masha flirted with Svistonov. Svistonov made jokes and told her gypsy fairy tales.

Masha became cross, reddened, and said that she was not a child.

"Poor Psikhachyov," Svistonov thought, walking out the door of the hospitable household.

"What a pity it's too late to drop in on Yablochkin." He looked at his watch. "Maybe I'll have a walk around the city." Having turned up his collar, Svistonov was off.

Yablochkin had a girlfriend. Her name was Antonina. Antonina worked in a candy factory and wore a red kerchief.

Yablochkin started corresponding with her in encryption, writing that he loved her and was ready to marry her. He wrote her all this in numerals. Yet there was no one from whom to conceal their love. They were both all alone.

In the evenings, the young man told her stories as they strolled along the undulating embankment or through the factory garden permeated by the smell of sweet essences. He had decided to introduce her to the cultured and congenial people living in the private house nearby. He thought that Svistonov and Psikhachyov lived together.

"How learned they are, Ninochka," he said. "It's even frightening. You drop in on them and they'll be sitting working on some kind of sketch with circles and rectangles. The older one will be explaining something to the younger one, who'll be listening and diligently writing things down."

"Oh look, here come our folk," Antonina said, smiling. "My gosh, how loudly they sing."

Groans of the guitar,
Songs of freedom and fields…
Where we'll forget our grief…
Hey, my chariot, yeah, chariot….

In the window above the garden appeared the two heads of Psikhachyov and Svistonov, one above the other.

"What's with this spectacle?" Svistonov inquired. "It sure is lively around here, Vladimir Yevgenyevich."

"Yes, this is the way it is every Saturday."

"Perhaps you'll play some Mozart, or maybe… whatever you like. Something from the past."

The window slammed shut.

Yablochkin stood with Antonina across from a lit-up window.

They could see the corner of the room with the antique portraits.

Vanya whispered: "So cozy in there. Such shelves, potted plants, stillness."

The music ceased.

Psikhachyov and Svistonov alighted from the porch, walked through the garden, and started off along the path.

"See here, dear Andrey Nikolayevich, it's as if you doubt the ancient origin of our order. You must believe…"

At the new moon, in a two-windowed room which Psikhachyov called the Capella, an academic meeting was being held. The antique portraits, as well as a freemasons' armchair bought at the Aleksandrovskiy Flea Market, had been moved in. The beds had been moved out.

Psikhachyov, wearing boots with spurs, a ribbon across his breast, sat at the place of the president, reading and interpreting selected passages from the Bible, the Seneca, Epictetus, Marcus Aurelius, and Confucius. On his right sat Svistonov; on his left, a former cavalry officer and Yablochkin; opposite him, a former prince, now an ice cream vendor.[5] After finishing the reading, Psikhachyov commenced asking his pupils in turn about the books they had read since the last scheduled meeting, about the observations or discoveries they had made, and about the efforts and labors they had extended for the expansion of the order—who were these people and in what respects they were fit for the order.

Yablochkin watched Psikhachyov intensely, trying his hardest to grasp it all.

The cavalry officer apparently was getting ready to raise an objection. He fidgeted impatiently in his chair.

Svistonov was bored and not completely at ease. It was starting to get absurd and bothersome to him that he was deceiving everyone.

In order to distract himself, he spilled matches onto the table, built a tower, then set it on fire. They all looked at him indignantly. "Why, they all positively believe Psikhachyov, they presume that a powerful order really exists. For all I know, he'll send a document to the Pope and, stranger things have happened, probably even receive money from America.

The order will blossom, and everyone will believe that it really existed all along."

"Brothers," continued Psikhachyov, "let us discuss the refinement of our spiritual abilities. Let us focus all our efforts on this. Let us develop the power of our thoughts. I am convinced that before long we will be able to move objects at a distance. Soon I will travel to the East to solicit blessings for you newly accepted brethren. There they will pray for us, and in our souls will be enlightenment and peace. Who wishes to submit questions? I shall do my best to bring you answers from the East."

The meeting dragged on well past midnight.

One evening Svistonov was sitting with Psikhachyov discussing Templars. A man with eyes bulging from his sockets entered; apparently he was suffering from exopthalmic goiter.

"Baron Medem," Psikhachyov introduced the arrival. Taking him aside, he gave his last ruble to the baron.

The baron bowed and vanished.

"You know, back then, in the 18th century, in the capacity of count, he welcomed me in his castle," Psikhachyov said gravely. "Pity you weren't there."

Svistonov smiled.

"Wait," said Psikhachyov. "Now I remember—you were there. You were wearing a lazuline camisole made of some kind of wondrous material. I remember, you gave me a ring with a carved stone."

"And you gave me this," Svistonov answered and withdrew from his pocket a ring with a heart, sword, and cross.

"That's exactly right!" exclaimed Psikhachyov. "How did I not recognize you?"

"Allow me to call you Count," said Svistonov. "After all, you're Count Phoenix and we're in Petersburg now."

"Of course, Baron," said Psikhachyov, grasping Svistonov by the arm. "We must drink to this occasion."

And they made a deep bow to each other.

Count Phoenix disappeared behind the portière. The sideboard creaked and vodka appeared.

"Olya, Olya!" Psikhachyov called out. "Bring in the tablecloth." Andrey Nikolayevich has turned out not to be Andrey Nikolayevich at all. It's him, my friend. Remember, I was telling you about him."

"Oh!" answered his wife.

Psikhachyov fussed about. A silver pepper mill from the 18th century apparently had disappeared somewhere.

"Run over to the cooperative," he said to his wife. "Tonight we dine by candlelight."

Psikhachyov and Svistonov had been reading the same books. The two friends' recollections were coinciding. The candles in the antique candlesticks cast tongue-like strips of light over the table set with antique flatware. The fruit from the LSPO Cooperative towered like a mountain on its silver plate.[6] The grapes glistened. The vodka was put aside and red wine appeared. Count Phoenix remembered how he was welcomed by Catherine II, said he was upset with his wife to this day. The host was playing the charlatan and thus at once looked at Svistonov to see if he, too, was playing a charlatan. Svistonov was truly overjoyed. He loved improvised evenings. He was lucky this evening.

"Tell me, Count," he asked, putting grapes in his mouth, "why were you incarnated as Psikhachyov?"

As he had not been on a tour for some time, Psikhachyov in the morning rolled out beads from a pasty mixture he had concocted, assembled necklaces, deliberated over earrings and brooches.

His wife was busy doing likewise, as was his daughter.

The pasty mixture was kept in tin cans meant for fruit drops and tea. On the table lay red, blue, white, orange, black, and green clumps. The wife tore off a green clump and turned it into an elongated little sausage by rubbing her palms together. The daughter cut this little sausage into equal-sized pieces, and Psikhachyov turned the pieces into beads. That is how fordism made its way into this quiet household. In the evening, Psikhachyov strung the beads onto thread and coated them with copal lacquer. In three or four days' time, he would sell them to his friends as well as to Gostinyy Dvor, calling them the latest novelty from Paris.

His daughter grew bored of the beads. She wanted her father to take her, at long last, to the secret ball where all the people wore colorful costumes. She wanted to watch her father win at cards in the secret gambling dens and then disperse the money to the needy. But meanwhile, instead of to grand balls, her father took her ever so rarely to the cinema and to the summer gardens, where she would guess what was in his pocket by means of a series of questions. Or else he took her to one of his magic performances, the ones after which he was obliged to give himself away, to reveal from the stage that it was all only sleight of hand while demonstrating how it was all done.[7]

Svistonov decided to take a break from Psikhachyov, to collect new material, to spend time on new characters. To let Psikhachyov rise in him like dough.

CHAPTER FIVE
GATHERING NAMES

Svistonov walked past the low white fence of the monastery, past the middle school, past the maternity house, through the gates, around the church and the small outer building with muslin-covered *fortochki*, and through another set of gates.[1]

He bent down before gravestones, looked up at angels with crosses, pressed his nose to the glass of crypts and inspected the insides. In front of him, relatives of the deceased were on their way to visit graves covered with chopped eggs and bread crumbs. Near the monument to the writer Klymov, he observed an old midget with a bouquet in his hands. The tiny old man put down his bouquet and dug reverently around a little grave, planting sticks in the ground and tying to them little flowers. Svistonov, touched by the scene, stopped momentarily. He continued on, peering into crypts as he went. In one crypt he saw a couple of vagrants. They were sitting on chipped iron sepulchral stools, playing cards. The crypt was locked from the outside.

A little old man was sitting atop a grave of a Japanese. Noticing that Svistonov was studying him intently, the old man explained:

"Nobody comes to visit him. I have nothing to do, so I come. I pity him."

Drunken people were lying picturesquely at a smallish grave. The least drunk one left and brought back a priest. He circled the others and removed their hats. The priest, glancing around, quickly began a service. When he finished, the half-drunk man paid him a recompense, circled the others, and replaced their hats. Then, addressing the grave, he pronounced with satisfaction:

"Well, Ivan Andreyevich, we have commemorated you pretty well in our prayers, we have drunk, we have completed a service. Certainly now you should be content."

Svistonov, having written it all down, was ready to carry on farther. But he caught sight of an acquaintance, a feulletonist, conversing with a priest not far from a graveside monument in the shape of a propeller. The feulletonist was making his face out to express hope, faith, love. He called the priest "father" and, seizing the moment, winked at Svistonov. Svistonov smiled.

After the priest, genuinely moved, had gone his way thinking that not all fine young people were yet extinct on this earth, Svistonov approached the feulletonist.

"Hunting?" he asked. "The hunt is a great matter."

"Yes, I want to portray life today with greater impact."

"And might you have any kind of material relating to..." Svistonov leaned towards the feulletonist's ear.

"I have, I have!" His face beamed. Gleefully lighting a cigarette, the feulletonist threw the match far off. "Only don't use him. I'm saving him for a certain adventure story."

"I'll redo him. I only need it as a detail, for general color."

"Listen!" The feulletonist's eyes flickered. He cast a glance around and, noticing an old woman, whispered in Svistonov's ear.

"And might you let me have you and the father?" asked Svistonov as they were finally parting. "I'll take the cemetery and the flowers and the two of you."

The feulletonist grimaced wryly.

"Andrey Nikolayevich," he said, "I never would have expected a dirty trick like that from you. I treated you with complete trust. And now you've betrayed my trust."

Svistonov, having parted company with the feulletonist, was enjoying the song of the birds, the meandering path of the railroad, the children playing *gorodki* behind the fence.

Pasha, pencil in hand, finally found him. They sat down, and Pasha began proposing to Svistonov surnames he had found in the cemetery.

"Your little story isn't bad," Svistonov remarked, remembering Pasha's manuscript. "Have you heard anything of Kuku?"

"Not a thing," Pasha answered.

"I tell you what, Pasha, give this note to Iya."

CHAPTER SIX
AN EXPERIMENT ON IYA

Iya came in the front entrance, walked through to the courtyard, ascended the back stairwell.

She pulled the doorbell, chimes rang out.

Svistonov, lying in wait for her, quickly threw open the door.

She walked cheekily into a half-lit entryway.

Iya had heard that Svistonov had interesting surroundings, that he lived by candlelight, that he kept magnificent gems and cameos in a special oak chest, that on the walls of his apartment hung extremely rare objects.

Reflected in the mirror was a flame from a candle. The cheap wallpaper caused Iya to writhe her shoulders disdainfully.

Svistonov helped the guest out of her coat and led her through the pitch dark dining room to the bedroom.

Iya believed that she knew everything and had the right to speak about everything, that she had the right to give her opinion on everything and to stick out her foot and assert that she was right.

Immediately Iya began striding around the room and stating her opinion of each object.

Surveying a varied selection of highly interesting treatises from the seventeenth century, she informed him that it must be Racine and Cornell and that she wasn't very fond of Racine and Cornell.

Glancing at Italian books from the sixteenth century, she remarked that it was pointless to concern oneself with these Horatiuses and Catulluses in this day and age.

Svistonov sat in the armchair and listened attentively.

He asked her opinion of the plate hanging on the wall.

Iya approached, took down the light blue plate bearing muscular little men and half-ram, half-triton figures, and announced proudly that she understood the meaning of these things—that it was, doubtlessly, a Danish wedding plate.

Satisfied with herself but not at all with Svistonov's surroundings and belongings, she sat down in a Venetian chair, taking it for a bad imitation of Moorish style.

"Would you like me to read you a chapter from my novel?" Svistonov asked.

Iya nodded her head.

"Yesterday I was thinking up a female character," Svistonov continued. "I took Maturin's *Melmoth the Wanderer*, Balzac's *The Magic Skin*, and Hoffmann's *The Golden Pot*, and concocted this chapter. Listen."

"Disgraceful!" Iya exclaimed. "Only in our uncultured country would it be possible to write by such means. Even I can do that! Frankly speaking, I don't really care for your prose. You neglect contemporary life. You might reply that I don't understand your novels, but if I don't understand, then who does? What kind of reader are you counting on?"

Taking her leave of Svistonov, Iya felt that she had not at all discredited herself, that she had shown Svistonov with whom he was dealing.

CHAPTER SEVEN
ARRANGING THE BOOKS

Svistonov had caught cold in the unheated apartment. His nose was inflamed and red. He had a slight fever. He decided to heat the stove, stay at home, and organize his neglected library. However, sorting books by section, as is well known, is a difficult task, for every kind of division is relative. Svistonov contemplated the kinds of sections into which to break down his books so that they would be easier to use at the given moment.

He divided the books by degree of nutritional value. First off, he started with the memoirs. For the memoirs he set aside three shelves. But along with the memoirs, after all, could be included the works of several great writers: Dante, Petrarch, Gogol, Dostoyevskiy. In the final analysis, it was all memoirs—memoirs, so to say, of spiritual experience. And then there were founders of religions, explorers.... And from a historical point of view, didn't physics, geography, history, and philosophy all serve as one gigantic memoir of mankind!

Svistonov didn't want to divide his books on a superficial basis. Everything for a writer is equally nutritious. Time—perhaps that was the sole principle. But to place a publication from 1573 with a publication from 1778 and 1906... his whole library would become a series of one and the same authors in various languages. A series of Homers, Vergils, Goethes. Undoubtedly it would end up having a harmful influence on his creativity. His attention could drift from characters to peripheral matters—dates of publication, commentaries, paper quality, bindings. He might find that kind of organization useful some day, but not now, while he was working on figures. Here sharp lines were needed. Here it was necessary to proceed not from interpretations but from things themselves. Interpretations, after all, must be only accompaniment. In order to establish a vast spectrum, Svistonov freed a shelf, took Gogol's *Dead Souls*, Dante's *Divine Comedy*, the works of Homer and other authors, and arranged them in a row.

"People are the same as books," thought Svistonov, taking a rest. "It's nice to read them. Most likely, they're even more interesting than books, richer. You can play with people, place them in all kinds of circumstances." Svistonov felt constrained by nothing.

CHAPTER EIGHT
THE SEARCH FOR SECONDARY FIGURES

Svistonov didn't stay at home long. His novel needed secondary figures, an air of the city, theatricality. The next day, towards evening, he went out.

With passion he took to transferring details of the city.

Invalids and a crowd of shoppers.

"Yes, yes," answered one who had bought some fowl. "I am the former Professor Nikolay Wilhelmovich Kirchner."

The professor still wore the same stained yarmulke, same flappy raincoat, same galoshes tied to his bare feet with string. Still the same glasses with gold rims, still the same everlasting bundle in his hand. Yet he still found it necessary to rush off and stand in all the endless lines.

Nowadays the professor received a pension of one hundred rubles and lived in the Bristol Hotel. But everything was over for him. Oblivion had befallen him. His face was sullen, his eyes reeled crazily, his lips were pursed slightly skeptically.

For ten years he and Svistonov had come across one another in the streets and had never exchanged words. But today the professor was feeling exceptionally distraught. He had been rudely tossed out of the administration offices of the State Philharmonic. He had been seized by the arms and thrown out onto the street, the door slamming in his face as he had turned around. How could it be! His sister, as it happened, had broken her leg on the stairs while leaving after a concert. She had slipped and fallen.

Bidding this peripheral figure farewell, Svistonov set off to his secondary figures, the old couple from Toksovo. The old couple were overjoyed at his presence, as they were lonely and loved to gab. To them it seemed that with Svistonov they could talk about their earlier life, could prove to him how musicians used to be valued, could show him the medal and the personally autographed picture of a high-ranking official and the portraits of high-ranking pupils, boys in full-dress military uniforms whom the old man taught to play balalaika in days of yore.

"Now, don't you fuss over me, Tatyana Nikandrovna, I'm a simple man," Svistonov said. "I like you both very much, and I simply dropped in to spend a little time together. How very homey it is here, Tatyana Nikandrovna. I feel it. I knew you would have homemade preserves. Now, of course I'm not the musician that Pyotr Petrovich is, but I do love music. And occasionally I really feel like hearing some music. I was even hoping that after tea Pyotr Petrovich might take out his flute and play some."

"And what do you play?" asked the old man.

"Oh, the piano, a little bit," Svistonov replied. "Just about with one finger. I can make out the notes, play accompaniments."

"You gave it up, that must be it?" asked the old man sympathetically. "Yes, there is little perseverance in people. Not one of my pupils became a musician. I remember I was teaching the children of a certain high-ranking civil servant. The boys were precious. These days they write that they treated people like us badly. Don't believe it, it's not true. Tatyana Nikandrovna can confirm it. What an upbringing they had! How they were taught to be mindful. At the slightest trouble, like that, their sweets were taken away or they were stood in the corner. And their mother would apologize and their father would come in and say, 'I'll punish them all right!' And never was I allowed to leave without joining them for dinner. What important people they were, yet they never failed to seat me beside them so as not to offend me...."

"And they recommended us," interrupted Tanya. "And found us lessons and good jobs, too."

"And that's to say nothing of the gifts," added the old man. "At Christmas as well as Easter. And if they knew you were getting married, without fail you had yourself a man to stand up for the bride. And if a son, then you had a godfather. And if your son turned out to be a revolutionary, the man himself would pay a visit to the commissioner."

Svistonov drank his tea, encouraged the old man to continue his storytelling. He asked questions, sighed here and there, listened attentively, shook his head back and forth, mumbled slightly, cleared his throat.

"I'll bring in the gifts and show you!" said the old woman.

"Petya, what have you done with the key?" she called from the next room.

Petya got up, and Svistonov heard the screeching of drawers being pulled open.

"My," said Svistonov tenderly, "does this little watch run?"

"Not only runs, but it strikes the hour." The old man was overjoyed. "Here, listen." He took a glass from the sideboard, turned it over, and placed the watch on top.

The watch distinctly struck eleven o'clock.

"Here's the little list first," said Tatyana, "telling what they gave us and when." She held out a yellowed piece of paper to Svistonov.

What wasn't on the list! Baskets of flowers with a visit card, a barometer, a cigarette case, cuff links, a tiepin.

Svistonov read on. The old couple disappeared for a moment, brought back their treasures, and said almost in a duet:

"We've saved all of it, nothing's been sold! We've gone hungry but never sold the things given to us." And on the table they spread out the gifts in front of Svistonov.

Svistonov was completely taken with the old couple. He decided that they were not completely secondary figures. He decided to drop in more often.

Returning by one and the same route, stopping to get a light and exchange a few words, Svistonov made friends with a militiaman.[1] The militiaman would read his verses:

At the tram track switches
Stands my Aglaya so tall,
The rail points she switches,
Her eyes on me never fall,
From my militiaman's seat,
I watch her lips so sweet....

At first the militiaman was afraid of something, but eventually he grew assured that Svistonov was a generally kind and conversant person.

Svistonov visited with the militiaman often, smoking and discussing poetry with him. They walked the streets together, their hands clasped behind their backs. The trees turned a blue hue, and the militiaman told about his village, how nice life was there, the heavenly apple trees, the kilos of dried apples they made at home from all the different kinds of *antonovka* apples, and how you could graft branches from a single apple tree onto a birch, an oak, or a linden and get distinctive tastes in the apples. He recounted how they produced formic acid, how they kept ants in small bags and pressed out the juice.

Svistonov inquired about the kinds of customs they had in the village, the superstitions, the local library, the sex lives of the young people. He asked the militiaman to recall it all, affirming that it was essential for his book.

They sat for long stretches on a bench beneath a gate. The militiaman talked about whatever popped into his head and answered Svistonov's questions. Svistonov wrote it all down by the light of the street lamp.

Much time passed. The old couple stood by their little window on the third floor. The sun shone like in a picture, the window open wide. The old man held Traviata by all four paws, and the old woman combed the dog's belly and tail with an ivory comb.

"Why so restless, Traviatochka?" the old woman said. "What are you barking and whimpering about? We mean you well. There, we'll scratch your neck. You can't get there with your teeth, after all. There, between the brows."

"Look how they nip at her," said the old man, moving the fur aside with his free thumb. "No wonder she's so sad."

"How I would like to see Nadenka's soul!" the old woman burst out for no apparent reason. "She probably has a wonderful soul."

"Yes, she is a discreet young lady. Scratch here. Obviously from a fine family. What do you think, will she marry Ivan Ivanovich? Don't fidget, Traviatochka!"

"Look out on the road, Traviatochka. Look who's over there. You see what a monster of a dog. They're walking it on a chain. Look, Traviatochka, look."

"But what a pity if she doesn't marry," said the old woman.

"Look how many there are! Stop, stop, one jumped on you!"

"Well, now how are you going to find it?"

"Remember how you used to wear that suit coat. And now you're not even clean shaven. Remember my satin dress with glass beads? There, you're clean now, Traviatochka. Let her down."

"Look how she shakes herself off!"

"Come on, Traviatochka, dance!" Taking the little dog by the paws, the old woman began leading it around her.

The pooch stepped slowly on its hind legs, from time to time lifted its head and yelped. Then the old woman took it in her arms, and the old pooch laid its head on her shoulder and closed its eyes, panting.

The old woman sang in a jingling voice:

Lullaby, and good night,
Lullaby, my little darling,
Come kitty, to spend the night,
Traviatochka will be rocking.

"Oh my aging darling! My poor thing, my balding little baby!" And the gray-haired little darling, having understood that she was being pitied, started to whimper morbidly.

The flutist's wife loved animals. She fed all the kittens on the stairs and cuddled the abandoned toms, outraged.

She had a woodshed in the courtyard. She practically lived in the shed.

Every hen and cock had its own name, either "my little girl" or "my little boy," and knew how to peck rolls from her hand. The old woman had goats, too.

Svistonov had burst right in on this peaceful family scene. He had picked up on the old woman's loneliness and rationalized it as the stifled anguish of motherhood. He began bringing treats for Traviatochka, started petting her and praising her. The old woman's heart opened completely.

"You see, everybody loves you," she said to Traviatochka.

"Everybody cares about you and everybody loves you very much! There now, just wait, come winter I'll knit you a new vest and you'll be an absolute beauty."

"Have you had the little dog long?" asked Svistonov.

"About six years," the old woman answered.

"She's not old at all."

"Of course. She's still a youngster," confirmed the old woman, having concealed the real age of her beloved pet.

"Won't you stay with us for dinner?"

Svistonov stayed.

Tatyana Nikandrovna sat Traviata on a chair, tied a napkin around her.

"Forgive us, please," said the old woman. "Traviatochka is like a little daughter to us."

They all sat down at the table and started with soup.

Traviatochka finished first, looked up at the others, whimpered. She loved to eat.

"Were you starving, Traviatochka?" asked Tatyana Nikandrovna.

Traviata listened, then whimpered again.

The old woman took Traviatochka's bowl, went to the kitchen, poured some more cold soup.

Traviatochka lapped it up again. Tatyana Nikandrovna brought in a roast and, for Traviatochka, on a separate plate with flowers, her very own piece with a bone. They drank tea, Traviatochka lapped milk. Then she jumped down from the chair and begged for a walk. After dinner Svistonov played accompaniment on the piano. The old man sat next to him and played the flute.

CHAPTER NINE
THE FIGHT AGAINST BOURGEOISIE

In the very same building lived Deryabkin.

Most of all on this earth Deryabkin feared vases. Deryabkin turned white at the word "bourgeois." That is why he did not allow his new wife to introduce into a room occupied by him any signs of femininity, such as geraniums and fuchsia. Additionally, he forbid her to hang a photograph of her mother on the wall. Despite his wife's resistance, he took the nail out of the wall and hid the hammer.

"If you want to live with me, then make an effort to submit to my will. I will not allow you to engage in such foolishness!"

And the next morning, Lipochka boarded the tram to take the houseplants back to her mother, who was washing Deryabkin's collars.

"Oh, those men, they don't like plants." She flung up her soapy hands.

They had lunch. Mother brought out the sheer curtains they had sewn for the windows.

Mother and daughter were filled with admiration. The sheer curtains had been homemade. Even Babushka had taken part sewing them.

"Look what I've brought, my darling little Pava!"

"I'm not Pava, I'm Pavel. Please don't call me by a dog's nickname."

"Look at these patterns...."

"Sheer curtains on the windows," Pavel stated dryly, "is a mark of bourgeois influence. I cannot allow it. We'll go to Passage on Saturday and buy something more fitting."

Svistonov, taking a walk along the streets, dropped into Passage to have breakfast.

Deryabkin, in spite of the crowd, walked proudly. Lipochka, holding onto her husband's sleeve, practically was running.

"Lookie there, a little vase! Couldn't we buy—"

"Stop, please, with your little vases."

"And there's a little kitten piggy bank."

"Stop pestering," said Deryabkin, irritated, freeing his sleeve. "And what's with this bourgeois manner of holding onto me? Walk along quietly."

"Buy us a picture, Pavochka. We'll hang it over our bed."

"I told you, stop pestering."

"Well then, buy us a lampshade."

"I'm not buying any lampshade."

Deryabkin made his fight the pearl of his existence. He did not sleep nights for thinking all the time how to guard against this evil. He would walk along the street and suddenly see on display in a store window a waxen bourgeoise. The bourgeoise would be dressed in tinsel, its bourgeois lips painted, its hair curled according to Paris fashion. "Well, hair salons, God help them, have always been this way, but cooperatives and state factory stores!"

It made Deryabkin's heart ache that bourgeois influences had penetrated the state factory stores.

"Such bad taste," uttered Deryabkin, scrutinizing a Murano glass vase, light as a feather.

"Indeed," corroborated Svistonov, stopping close by. "It's nice to see a man who understands these things."

"What kind of fish is that?" asked Lipochka, turning around.

"A dolphin," answered Svistonov.

"She's constantly dreaming about goldfish!" explained Deryabkin to the man with whom they were familiar from frequent run-ins in their courtyard.

The familiar man moaned sympathetically. Deryabkin, sensing unexpected support, was greatly pleased.

"See, I told you. The citizen also confirms it."

"Why, yes, it falls upon everyone to fight against bourgeois influences," sighed Svistonov, hiding his smile in his collar.

This was, apparently, a knowledgeable and educated man.

"Perhaps you wouldn't mind advising us—I believe we've run into each other in the yard—on a purchase?" Deryabkin asked the stranger. "I'm Pavel Deryabkin, accountant."

"Svistonov, literator."

"That's fine," said Deryabkin. "You see, Lipochka, a literary man has the same opinion."

Deryabkin, having loaded up Lipochka—he believed men were not supposed to carry shopping bags—took hold of Svistonov.

"Come over to our place for tea."

Svistonov followed Deryabkin and Lipochka down to their basement apartment.

On the floor lay a red and black cloth runner, the kind formerly found in front entrances. There was also a dining table along with a mirror taken from a front entrance. Unusual cleanliness ruled the basement. The windows looked almost like crystal; the window sills had been polished to a shine. The floor, painted yellow, sparkled.

"Hygiene," said Deryabkin, "is the first sign of culture. Here, look how our toothbrushes are arranged." And Deryabkin led Svistonov to the little shelf above the sink. "See, and the soap is also in a case, so no bacilli turn up. On this front I have already won. Now a new front has opened for me. Now, in the evenings, I work on handwriting. Calligraphy trains a person to be assiduous and patient."

The literate and cultured man was for Deryabkin a supreme guest. The host thirsted for enlightenment. Deryabkin not only worked on handwriting in the evenings. Besides that, he listened to the radio. The radio brought Deryabkin to a state of rapture. He believed that, thanks to the radio, he could be abreast of everything on earth. He could become enlightened about opera and wouldn't have to waste time on the tram. And what economy! He often spoke about this with his wife. And there was trouble if his wife made any noise while he sat wearing his shiny earphones.

Lipochka also decided to make a credible showing.

"I'm so anemic that my only saving grace is dreaming. I can fall asleep whenever I want and sleep for as long as I want," Lipochka, seating herself on the small multi-colored sofa, related to Svistonov.

"How did you learn to fall asleep whenever you want?" Svistonov, leaning against the back of the sofa, inquired.

"Working nights teaches you everything," sighed the hostess.

"You're so refined," Svistonov uttered sadly. "It must be difficult for you to bother with the housekeeping."

"I have to run all over the place," replied the hostess. "If it keeps up like this for much longer, I'll die. And all the fuss with the bindings! Practically every day I've been running to the book bindery."

"What bindings?" Svistonov grew curious.

The hostess proudly led the guest to the little etagere.

"These are my Pavel's favorite books."

Svistonov bent down. *The Old Days*, the yearbook of the Architectural Society.

"You have a keen understanding of the arts," said Svistonov, straightening himself. "These cloth bindings are uncommonly suited to your decor."

It was at this point that Andrey Nikolayevich decided to become one of the family.

In the apartment began to be heard: "Andrey Nikolayevich said... Andrey Nikolayevich recommended... Andrey Nikolayevich got us tickets to a concert tonight.... Andrey Nikolayevich is taking us to a museum...."

The old couple upstairs grew jealous.

"Has Andrey Nikolayevich taken offense at us?" they wondered.

Deryabkin's social circle consisted of the following:

The spinster Pluchard, a seventy year-old retired class mistress with a braid wound around the back of her head and two teeth on her upper jaw, a spinster for whom by this time there was nowhere left to go to dance the mazurka. And how dashingly she had danced in her yellow laced shoes at those balls of yesteryear, in the same gymnasium she trod by morning with her arms folded across her chest and a stony countenance, crying out, "There's time for work and time for play!"

The hairstylist Jean, an educated man, a lover of neatness, to whom it now fell upon to shave and cut the hair of—the devil only knows the kind of people![1] Clients with whom it was impossible to even talk, with whom it was impossible to exchange stories, who were incapable of imparting a single thing! Whereas before to cut hair and shave faces was a singular pleasure. One knew what was going on in the Senate, what was happening abroad, how the evening at the home of Countess Z. went off. The hairstylist Jean had been received in the best households in the city. On the day of his patron saint, he used to don a top hat and coat. And what a singular pleasure taking communion was in those days. Full-dress uniforms spun from gold, white trousers, three-pointed caps held beneath arms, swords, lightly colored dresses, the smell of perfumes and eaux de cologne, friends and acquaintances. You stood near the doorway and just managed to exchange bows.

Vladimir Nikolayevich Golod, the owner of the Decadence Photographic Studio, where all those being photographed had to fix their eyes and assume wooden looks.

And the former contractor Indyukov, a great drunk and an enemy of the people.

This entire society got along very well, almost gaily.

Indyukov respected the spinster Pluchard as an erudite and intelligent woman. The spinster Pluchard regarded Indyukov as a good man albeit a drunk one. The spinster's ideas on upbringing and those of the widowed old man did not completely coincide. To Indyukov, however, it seemed that their ideas coincided completely, which made him glad.

Jean, although beneath Pluchard by background, during his life had acquired manners, knew several French words of the kind necessary to a hairstylist of his day, and knew all there was to know about the theatrical world. So Pluchard, albeit too late, had a chance to learn about life behind the scenes.

There was, of course, in this society also a former officer, as there is in practically every society. Who, after all, had not served in the relatively recent past? He had been mobilized when still a moustacheless youth, and to this day he carried the rank of an officer. He had achieved notoriety for his mazurka when still a first-year student at the Geology Institute.

Now Malvin was a completely lonely man. That is why he loved Deryabkin very much.

Everybody knows lonely people. Everybody knows that they can be sheepish and occasionally merry in a nervous way and that they love to recall that bygone time when they sparkled.

On Sundays and holidays, the entire society assembled in Deryabkin's apartment. Svistonov had become part of this society. Svistonov did not miss a single Sunday.

Pluchard had respect for literature and believed that literature should instruct in a straightforward manner. Jean liked humorous short stories. Indyukov said that books were not for his kind of mind. Malvin preferred popular science novels. There were things for them to talk and argue about.

They had got the spinster Pluchard tipsy. She sat, red and animated, in her shortened skirt and collared blouse buttoned to the top. Indyukov was intoxicated and had become garrulous. Malvin kept pouring a glass for Svistonov from a bottle and asking his opinion on literature.

Deryabkin wanted to exhibit his friends to Svistonov in all their glory so that Svistonov would know with whom he, Deryabkin, was acquainted.

"Anna Nikolayevna will dance a mazurka," he said to Svistonov. "She has been shy in front of you up to now, but today I think it's all right."

And what transpired, from Svistonov's point of view, was something picturesque. The guests and the host moved the table aside. Deryabkin took a guitar and began to play. Everyone, with the exception of Pluchard and Malvin, took a seat along the wall. Malvin approached Pluchard, inviting her to dance. He clasped her behind the waist, and they galloped off on the small clearing. Malvin outlined a pas, trying his best to dance as when he was a student, coming to rest on one knee. The spinster Pluchard galloped around him. He jumped up, spun her one more time, and off they galloped.

Svistonov had been taking it all in: Pluchard's tousled braid, the blue veins on her temples, the slightly disdainful and prim look on her face; Malvin's bald spot and perspiration; the colorful figure of the bearded Indyukov, dozing good-naturedly in the corner; the bamboo summer chairs; the chintz-upholstered couch made up of a mattress and a long egg crate. For Svistonov, people did not divide into good and evil, pleasant and unpleasant. They divided into necessary for his novel and unnecessary. This society was necessary, and he felt perfectly at home in it. He did not compare himself to Zola, who retained even surnames, nor to Balzac, who wrote and wrote and then went out to meet people, nor to his acquaintance N., who one day tried to indict himself of a Smerdyakov-like transgression just to see what kind of impression it would create.[2] He took for granted that it was all quite excusable for an artist and that there would be a reckoning for it all some day. But he did not think about what kind of reckoning awaited him; he lived one day at a time, without bothering about tomorrow. He was immersed in the very process of abducting people and transferring them into a novel.

He sensed strongly the parodiable nature of the world with respect to any kind of norm. "Instead of by a proper meter inscribed in our souls," the poet might say, "the world moves according to its own original rhythm." Svistonov, however, was already past those years of aspiring to find answers to the world's questions. He wanted to be an artist, that is all. From the poet's standpoint, Svistonov possessed Mephistopheles-like traits. But Svistonov, truthfully, did not see these qualities in himself. On the contrary, everything to him was simple, clear, and natural.

The poet would not be at a loss. The poet would object that this is exactly a Mephistopheles-like quality, a Mephistopheles-like stance, this disdainful and disagreeable attitude towards the world, in no way whatsoever inherent to the artist. But then, that is what being a poet is all about: expressing oneself with high style and opacity, searching for some kind of correlation between the attendant world and the nether world. Svistonov was a sober-minded individual and, from all indications, possessed sufficient will power to stay his course.

The world to Svistonov had long ago become a *kunstkammer*, a collection of fascinating monstrosities and freaks, and he was something like the director of this *kunstkammer*.[3]

Deryabkin's workday consisted of visiting apartments. Strictly speaking, not apartments, but rather apartment entryways, where such were to be had. It was his job to write down how much electricity was used each month and by whom. Deryabkin was a man with an open mouth and a crew-cut hairstyle.

The spinster Pluchard's workday consisted of wiping noses, conducting French conversations, and if the weather was fair, visiting public gardens with children and little dogs. She would walk through a garden dragging along a child, saying, "C'est qu'on ne connait le prix de la santé que lorsqu'on l'a perdue. Repeat, Nadya." And Nadya would mince along behind her, repeating. The spinster Pluchard hated children and had no interest in her surroundings.

Deryabkin loved taking up anti-religious topics with Ivan Prokofyevich.

"Your religion," he would say, "is a lie and an opiate. You haven't read any books, Ivan Prokofyevich."

Deryabkin tried to out-argue Ivan Prokofyevich and assume superiority over him. But the gray-haired Jean would not give in. He would recall the words of a high-ranking civil servant, a great thinker, sitting at home in front of a mirror and telling Jean, who was shaving him carefully: "The matter isn't flaws in the priesthood, but in the idea...."

On weekday evenings Deryabkin treated his guests to the radio. Lipochka poured tea, and the guests ate and drank while a woman's voice sang gypsy romances, the languorous sighs of Hawaiian guitars tickled their ears, verses were recited, and the music of Danish or other composers was performed. Occasionally they listened to an opera in its entirety.

Deryabkin himself fashioned a loudspeaker out of cardboard and lacquered it. The black tube stood atop the table beside homemade preserves, crying out and singing and laughing and transmitting the sweetest sounds.

CHAPTER TEN
THE TEENAGER AND THE GENIUS

Mashenka hurriedly placed the lamp on the mirror-stand and opened the door.

"My God, Andrey Nikolayevich, how pale you are! Why, you're soaked to the bone! After a brief pause, she asked, "Do you like milk? We've got cream today!"

She snatched off Svistonov's overcoat and carried it away to the kitchen. Then she pulled Svistonov into the dining room. Smiling, she rushed to the sideboard and dotingly held a crystal milk jar in front of the guest's nose. Svistonov was overcome with admiration.

"Vladimir Yevgenyevich isn't home?" he asked.

"No, Papa went out on business." And she went about looking in the sideboard for the little cup her father had given her on her name-day.

"Go on, drink up already!" she exclaimed, sitting Svistonov down and offering him her favorite cup.

Svistonov took a sip.

"Only, don't go, it's frightening being here alone."

"But the thing is, I only stopped by for a minute..." replied Svistonov.

Seeing how Mashenka's face had changed, he cut himself short.

"But if you're frightened, I'll happily stay."

Gusts of wind shook the little house with its two lit-up windows. The storm was supposed to worsen towards nightfall.

"Probably nothing will be left of our oak tree," Mashenka said, only now remembering that she still had newspaper in her hair.

She quickly took off the paper and threw it into the fireplace.

"Sit down over here for a minute, Andrey Nikolayevich."

Mashenka left and returned with an armful of marvelously dried birch firewood intended for kindling. She threw it down and went about ripping off the bark.

Svistonov began chopping up the sticks with a knife.

"Your socks are soaking wet. Would you like me to bring Papa's slippers?"

Svistonov sat wearing Psikhachyov's slippers. He had grown unaccustomed to young people and did not know how to treat them. Moreover, it embarrassed him that nobody else was in the house other than him and Mashenka.

He sighed with relief when Mashenka took the initiative to make conversation yet noticed that he himself was answering the teenager vacuously and sluggishly, despite his kind intentions. He even began to despair over the fact that he had not a word nor a thought for Mashenka.

She had already read somewhere that a writer was a lofty and clever being, that a writer possessed a majestic nature which defied time and penetrated the secret that was written on everyone's faces. It was this very secret that Mashenka was desirous of penetrating.

She very much wanted Svistonov to read her his new novel. She knew that the guest carried it with him wherever he went, like some priceless object.

What's more, Psikhachyov had once told her that Svistonov was a genius; and the word genius carries with it, and will likely never lose, a particular magnetic force. Mashenka wanted to talk candidly with Svistonov, to have a heart-to-heart talk with a genius.

Svistonov felt obliged to keep up the conversation.

"How wonderful it would be to marry a genius, to free a genius from petty daily concerns!" she thought.

And Mashenka decided to feed the unspeaking genius dinner.

She leapt up from the couch, opened the *fortochka,* and began rummaging around between the storm windows.

Psikhachyov's household was a poor one, however, and she found only a piece of salted pork fat and a large glass jar of sauerkraut.

Heartened, she ran after a frying pan.

The pork fat sizzled, the cabbage browned by the minute, and not all of the delicious aroma escaped through the flue. Mashenka even found vodka.

The genius drank and ate, and Mashenka, enraptured, sat opposite him.

The genius finished, placed his napkin aside, and lit a cigarette.

Svistonov grew pensive. He was thinking about how the food had smelled of smoke and where and when was it that the food had also smelled of smoke.

Mashenka watched and, still not depleted of admiration, asked the genius to read his novel.

"No, Mashenka," said Svistonov. "Come now."

But then it began to interest Svistonov what kind of impression his novel would make on a teenager and whether or not, in general, a teenager would be able to read his novel.

Svistonov went to the entry and brought back the rolled-up manuscript. He thought for a while, thought some more, and began reading.

From the first lines, it seemed to Mashenka that she had entered a strange world, barren, ugly, and sinister, an empty space with talking figures. And among these talking figures she suddenly recognized her father.

He was wearing an old greasy cap, had the enormous nose of a punchinello. In one hand he was holding a magic looking glass…

CHAPTER ELEVEN
THE LITTLE STAR AND SVISTONOV

Svistonov read:

On branches songbirds singing out
To praise the gifts of gracious God;
And love accords their operetta,
And love rejoices in their hearts.

Little meek lambs milling about
Nibbling the grass in the meadows,
Their hearts graze, full of love for God;
In wordless language they thank Him.

Lying light-hearted on the grass,
The shepherd playing his reed pipe
Breathes life from nature's ambrosia
And praises springtime's sublimity.[1]

At last Svistonov came to a rough representation of an old man and woman:

It does the heart good to look at the little old women...

He was altering pages from an 1842 childrens book entitled *The Little Star*:

as they saunter about the garden not thinking of anything save the flowers and the trees, the birds and the blue heavens; it does the heart good to look at the little old women as they tie their caps and their capes as needed and prance and delight in the fresh air and the green grass like God's little birds.

There once was...

Svistonov continued altering:

...a little old woman who was loved by everyone who knew her. When dogs saw her, they began barking with joy and licking her hands. Cats meowed and rubbed against her leg, while little kittens jumped about and started playing with her. And why did everyone love the little old woman so? Because she was kind and gentle and like a mother to them. She often sat on the rug and fed piroshki to her little dog. She herself loved piroshki, but was ever ready to hand them over to Traviata, and Traviatochka loved her for that. The little old woman's name was Sasha.

Every Sunday she attended obednya, *and one had to admire how still she stood and zealously she prayed.*[2] *Her eyes gazed incessantly upon the icons in front of her and never off to the left or to the right or even to the rear like those of naughty boys and girls sometimes do. She asked to be made kind and God-fearing. She asked that health and happiness be sent to her husband, to Traviatochka, and to all people on earth. Because of these thoughts, the time for her passed so quickly that she never felt fatigued during the* obednya *like the other little old women and men to whom* obednya *often seemed very long. How nice to behold an old woman so humble, so quiet. She was attentive and attendant to the younger ones and gentle towards all people in her house. If she had to borrow something, a pan or an iron, she did so sweetly and with such humility that it was impossible to refuse her the favor. And the old woman blushed at the slightest compliment.*

Sometimes in the evenings, if her husband was away, which happened very rarely, she opened her trunk and took out various bits of clothing, pieces of embroidery, Easter eggs, pencil stubs, old opera posters and programs, once-fashionable pictures, congratulatory postcards, envelopes, visit cards. She looked over the pages of calendars and read verses:

Sunshine blazes so brightly,
Air is blowing oh so warm,
And the public strolls rightly
'Round Gostinyy Dvor they swarm;
All these wondrous little treats,
Sparkling, heaping on the counters—
Willows, tiny bells, dolls, and sweets…

And she recalled the willow branches all around Gostinyy Dvor.[3]

Svistonov closed the book wondering where to insert this excerpt, how to tie it to the whole novel, and whether or not to compose the introduction right away. Again he took up the book that he had just laid aside, opened it to the bookmark, and changing one word for another, wrote out a page:

Introduction

It's nice to read an interesting book. Behind one, you don't notice time passing. Isn't this true, dear readers? And you, I believe, have already many times in your life felt this, although you have not yet had time to read a great deal. But have you noticed what kind of books you like best? Of course, those in which everything that is written about is put simply, clearly, and truthfully. For example, if it is some kind of flower being written about, then this flower is described so well and so much in accordance with what it actually is that upon seeing it you immediately recognize it from its description, even though you have never seen it before; if it is some kind of small woodland being written about, then it is as if you see its every tree, as if you feel the coolness its shade brings to the earth warmed by the summer sunshine; and if people are described in such a book, then it is as if they are alive right in front of you. You recognize their facial features, expressions, habits. It seems to you that you would immediately recognize them were they able to actually appear before you.

And however many decades and even centuries pass after the creation of this book, still its descriptions will remain beautiful because they are done truthfully to nature.

Thus I begin this tale of mine, which will trickle like a peaceful rivulet through banks strewn with silvery daisies and sky-blue forget-me-nots.

In the morning, having reread the chapters and materials, Svistonov confirmed that in the novel there were no gardens. No gardens whatsoever. Not new, not old. No workers gardens, no city gardens. But without greenery, a novel cannot exist, just as a city itself cannot.

Svistonov went out to work; the day was perfectly suited. He walked past the monument to Peter the Great but turned around upon hearing singing. A gray-bearded man in a long coat which had turned green was coming from Senate Square, getting closer to the monument. He stopped before the monument and shook his fist at Peter:

We gave you our bread—
And you brought us wigs.
All pogroms come from you.

Then he lowered his head and wandered on.

Svistonov stopped and wrote it all down, then entered the Workers Garden. He bought cigarettes and a chocolate from an invalid, lit up, and began carefully examining the condition and location of the garden. "What to abstract from it? Perhaps the busts in their uniforms? Perhaps take the people sitting on the ledge of the fountain pool? Or maybe depict the Admiralty with its gigantic figures? The people crowding, whirling, courting one another?"

Svistonov leaned against a tree trunk.

Three o'clock in the morning. A bar. Svistonov took a seat right next to the orchestra. On the stage a trio was playing: on violoncello, an old timer in a velvet jacket; on violin, a Russian in a gray suit and gaiters; on piano, a stuttering Jew.

Sounds whined out:

Don't tempt me without reason…

An old man rose from his table. An authoritative gesture—"Keep quiet!"—directed at his drinking companion, a young man in a *kosovorotka* and black leather gloves.[4] And then, listening to the melancholic romance, the old man covered his eyes with his hand and began to weep.

"The soul of Don Juan is inside him," thought Svistonov, and not without impatience remembered that in his pocket were the gardens only recently secured.

Home again. The candle had burned down, the wick lay on its side with the flame touching the candlestick cup.

Svistonov took out a railroad candle and placed it in the candlestick. He lit a cigarette, thought a while, and grabbing from his pocket the piece of paper with the gardens now transposed into words, he hunched over. Then he placed Psikhachyov in one of these gardens:

Having finished the reading, Psikhachyov approached an old man's table.

"Your fate is horrible," he told the old man in his ear.

Psikhachyov worked evenings in the taverns in the capacity of a handwriting analyst. He approached with compassion, yet by habit his vocal chords added:

"Would you care to give a sample of your handwriting?"

The old man pulled his hand away from his face and glared at Psikhachyov.

Music resounded from the Summer Theater. A few acorns had fallen onto the path. The tree-tops, darker than the trunks ablaze with tiny electric lights of various colors, brushed against one another.

CHAPTER TWELVE
THE MANUSCRIPT COMES TOGETHER

Stacks of spontaneous drawings, clippings, notes, phrases overheard in shops ("this lamb is like a mirror, the fat like snow!"), conversations ("all that I do is drink tea or coffee..."), observations ("an older man with a paunch, sitting at a table, meowing in order to expresses his wish to have tea"), genre scenes, sketches of various parts of the city—all of this was growing and coming to cohesion in Svistonov's room.

A corps of half-alive characters had to be discarded; many characters, coinciding with one another in certain extraordinary ways, had to be fused into one; secondary ones as well, and even those from a third group; a fourth batch had to be retained as a general background, a crowd in which a head, shoulder, arm, or back would flash.

Svistonov yawned and put down his fountain pen. Layers of dust had already managed to settle on his books since the recent rearrangement, and crumbly little beetles and slimy little bugs nibbled, gnawed, and bored at the books. The bugs made a ticking sound, competing with the clock. To the music of the bugs Svistonov drew himself up. "What should I do?" he wondered. He decided to take a stroll. He walked along the street, fatigued by work, his mind empty, his soul aired.

The novel was finished. First had come the gardens, the characteristic buildings, the soft sunrises, the noises and general din of the streets. Then names popped up here and there; they met and shook hands, played chess or cards, disappeared and re-appeared. With the names, figures started to appear. And finally, to each name rose a person.

It had all been permeated by a sweet, plaintive, captivating rhythm, as if the author had attempted to lure someone away with him.

The author no longer wanted anything to do with it. But his creation haunted him. It started to seem to Svistonov that he was inside his novel. Here he runs into Kukureku on some kind of strange street, and Kukureku calls out, "Kuku, Svistonov, Kuku! You are Kuku, Svistonov!"

Suddenly, out of Kuku jumps Psikhachyov. In a deserted area he begins performing his sorcery. "Here," he says, "now I will show you how to enter into a pact with the devil. But for God's sake, don't tell Mashenka about it. What's this, you're talented? You're a genius? Will you portray me to the world with all of my evil power?" And Psikhachyov begins pronouncing the words, "Sarabanda, puhanda, rasmeranda…" And Svistonov sees himself beneath a full-leafed birch tree telling Mashenka about her father. "That's the way it is, Mashenka," he says, "your father is not any kind of outstanding man at all but rather some sort of despicable and despised individual. He's no real mystic, the devil only knows what he is. He can't see past his own nose. As to those glasses he uses to see the invisible world, well, you know, it's a slightly… well… he never had any such glasses. So there's no way he could have lost them. He lied about receiving them from a certain German professor. He lied about using them to see his ancestors having dinner." And Mashenka is somehow not fourteen years old but rather eighteen. And here, in single file, comes Pasha and the police officer and the deaf girl.

Svistonov went out.

"Dee, dum… hey, my chariot, yeah… dee dah, dah dee dah… they parted like ships on the sea." House-lanterns lit up the corners of buildings and their gates. The sounds of songs and guitars drifted out into the alleys only to return to the embankment and fade between the stars and their reflections.

In the daytime, from up above, the city gave the impression of a toy city. The trees didn't seem planted but rather arranged; the houses, not erected but rather placed, the people and the trams, mechanical.

At night, on the Fontanka Embankment, Svistonov smoked cigarettes above the upside-down illuminated buildings. The long, cast-iron grillwork of the handrails shimmered in the water; the clouds swam illuminated by the hidden moon.

Solitude and boredom showed on Svistonov's face. The flames in the water, which had so captivated him in childhood, no longer amused him.

He felt everything around him thinning with each day. Places he had described were turning into vacant lots for him; people with whom he had been acquainted were losing all interest for him.

Each of his characters had siphoned off an entire array of people; each description had turned into something like the conception of an entire range of places.

The more he deliberated over his newly published novel, the greater was the rarefaction, the greater was the emptiness taking shape around him.

At last he felt he was completely locked inside his novel.

Wherever Svistonov showed up, he saw his characters all around. They had different names, different bodies, different hair, different manners, but he recognized them right away.

Svistonov had crossed over into his creation altogether.

NOTES

INTRODUCTION

The Introduction is based on T.L. Nikolskaya's introduction to *The Goat Song* (Moscow: Sovremennik, 1991).

[1] Christened "St. Petersburg" by its founder, Peter the Great, Russia's capital from 1712–1917 was renamed the less Germanic-sounding Petrograd in 1914 and then re-renamed Leningrad upon Lenin's death in 1924. In 1991 its citizens voted on a referendum to reclaim its original name; today it is St. Petersburg once again.

[2] History has bought into the Soviet propaganda machine by using the term "Bolshevik Revolution" to refer to what was actually a coup d'etat. Although Russian society was indeed revolutionized, the Bolsheviks were a minority party in the democratic Constituent Assembly which was formed after the tsar's abdication. They ultimately took power by force, not by virtue of popular will, sparking years of bloody civil war and debilitating famine throughout Russia.

CHAPTER ONE

[1] Throughout the novel Vaginov punctuates his cinematic prose with Soviet jargon, emphasizing its penchant for incongruous compounds—in this case *Molokosoyuz*, or milk union. A milk union, in fact, was nothing more than a dairy shop. Its new moniker likely was as absurd to Vaginov,

who already was an educated young man by the time of Soviet cultural revolution, as it is to us today.

[2] Vaginov gives a detailed description of the view from his apartment on the Griboyedova Canal.

[3] Renamed to honor the Bolshevik coup d'état, this street originally was and is today called Nevskiy Prospect. It is the main boulevard of St. Petersburg.

[4] In fact, Svistonov's creativity epitomizes a systematic process. This will already be clear by Chapter Three, when Svistonov is able to "get down to his systematic creativity."

[5] Svistonov's train of creative thought is interrupted by a sarcastic remark, as he imagines his imaginary exotic character with the ubiquitous Soviet job title "engineer."

[6] Present day Liteynyy Prospect. In Vaginov's time, it was a row of secondhand booksellers. Some of them survive today.

[7] *Gostinyy Dvor*: St. Petersburg's main department store, located on Nevskiy Prospect.

[8] Vaginov himself disdained electricity, and it was only installed in his apartment by an electrician roommate in the early 1930s.

[9] Lenochka is reading Matvey Komarov's *The Tale of the Adventures of English Lord George and of Brandenburg Margrave Frederick Louis* (1782). The book was reprinted in cheap popular print up until 1917. In 1930 Vaginov gave his copy to the House of Writers library.

[10] Vaginov parodically describes a theatrical evening of the OBERIU circle of writers and artists entitled "Three Left Hours" which took place at the Leningrad House of Publishing on 24 January 1928. Vaginov himself took part, reading to the accompaniment of an improvised dance by ballerina M. Popova.

11 Originally called *Tsarskoye Selo*, or Tsar's Village, this suburb of St. Petersburg, where several royal palaces are located, was renamed *Detskoye Selo*, or Childrens Village after the Bolshevik coup d'état. Famed and beloved as the place where Pushkin attended lyceum, the town today is called Pushkin.

12 It is obviously still a bit strange to Vaginov that once revered royal palaces suddenly had been converted into "museums."

13 That is, the Lyceum of Tsarskoye Selo where young Pushkin studied from 1811–1817 and first stood out as a talented writer of poetry.

14 Those owning, renting, or otherwise spending time at a dacha. The dacha, or country cottage, practically is a Russian national institution, with many city dwellers heading to dacha during the summer months.

15 From this park in front of the St. Petersburg Admiralty, Svistonov is able to see (and Vaginov describes) not only the Admiralty, but also the Palace Bridge (then renamed the Republican Bridge), the Imperial Winter Palace (then renamed the Palace of Arts), and Palace Square.

CHAPTER TWO

1 Another Soviet-coined compound, the word *kultprosvetchitsa* literally means "cultural educator." That this *kultprosvetchitsa* suggests such a comparatively mundane activity as a game of tag is characteristic of the sarcasm underlying the narrative.

2 The architectural style Vaginov refers to has been dubbed "Stalinist Gothic." Although its chief examples are seven unmistakable skyscrapers planted around downtown Moscow, the style also was widely used throughout Russia, incongruously to be sure, for rural train depots and riverboat stations.

3 In fact, never again in the narrative is the dog called "old girl"; she is always called by her name or by a diminutive.

[4] Literally "little cities." The game, called *ryukhi* in the original text, revolves around an arrangement of small stumps called *ryukhi* which are displaced from their 'little cities,' or *gorodki,* by throwing sticks.

[5] The Russian word for church here is *kirka* ('kirk' in English), thus distinguishing it from a Russian Orthodox church.

[6] Vaginov does not refrain from the tradition of endowing characters' surnames with ironic meaning. *Svistonov* is created from the root *svist,* or 'whistle.' More significantly, the verb form, *svistet,* is a colloquialism for the act of petty thievery, along the lines of the English 'to snatch,' or 'to sneak off with.'

[7] Following Russia's withdrawal from World War I and the subsequent Bolshevik coup d'état, bloody civil war and consequential debilitating famine ravaged the country for more than three years. Kuku comments on the state of St. Petersburg and its denizens during that time.

[8] Vladimir Yakovlevich Kurbatov (1878–1957), a prolific writer on the artistic history and landscape artistry of St. Petersburg and its environs.

[9] From the poem "The Devil's Swings" (1907) by Fyodor Sologub.

[10] Another surname with different referential layers. In a looser system of transliteration, the name might be rendered something like "Psychachev." The reader should know that the Russian root *psikh* corresponds to the English "psych."

CHAPTER THREE

[1] Nowadays incorporated into the Hotel Astoria, the Angleterre was temporary residence to a number of celebrated performers and writers, including poet Sergey Yesenin, who, according to official accounts now greatly in doubt, hung himself in his room in 1925.

[2] Yelagin, Kamennyy, and Krestovskiy Islands, located in the northern part of St. Petersburg, were favorite recreation destinations for city

residents at the beginning of the 20th century. They still feature popular parks and beaches today.

[3] From Pushkin's *Yevgeniy Onegin*.

[4] The estate, located outside of Moscow, where Lev Tolstoy spent most of his life.

[5] A *spletnik*, literally, is a gossip. Vaginov has every intention of not softening this term, of giving these young literary fans this rather caustic label usually reserved for idle old women. He repeats the term so many times, however, using both gender forms as well as the plural, that to use the English equivalent would result in an overbearing and distracting clumsiness not felt in the Russian.

[6] One-time exile and final resting place of Aleksandr Pushkin.

CHAPTER FOUR

[1] There is no mistaking Vaginov's use of the word *prozrachen*, meaning transparent, to describe the house. It is an uncommon usage, perhaps referring to Svistonov's dream in Chapter One, perhaps indicating the house's ability to reveal the personality of its owner.

[2] In Russian fairy tales, the cottage of Baba Yaga, the prototypical witch, stands on hens' legs, enabling it to turn around. Its usual position is facing the woods, away from the footpath running by it.

[3] *adarmapagon … mederme*. Hellenistic abracadabra.

[4] See final note of Chapter Two.

[5] Literally a "prince-ice cream man" (*knyaz-morozhenshchik*). Such were common, unavoidably ironic epithets marrying a person's status before the Bolshevik coup d'état with his new station in Soviet society.

6 The Leningrad Allied Consumer's Society Cooperative. Another typical Soviet designation, this time for a food store.

7 Under the Soviet regime, Psikhachyov is required to betray himself so as not to propagate beliefs in such things as magic, which were strictly contrary to the Bolshevik's primitive materialism.

CHAPTER FIVE

1 A *fortochka* is a small, hinged pane of window usually opened for ventilation.

CHAPTER EIGHT

1 After the Bolshevik coup d'état, even the name *politsiya* ('police') was considered too connected with capitalistic traditions and therefore was changed. Hence to this day Russia's police forces, while not at all associated with a militia per se, nonetheless are called *militsiya* ('militia').

CHAPTER NINE

1 Obviously not his real name but rather his career name. His real name, as we later learn, is Ivan Prokovyevich.

2 That is, Dostoyevskiy's Smerdyakov from *The Brothers Karamazov*.

3 Peter the Great founded the St. Petersburg Kunstkammer to display his collection of human and animal anomalies and other curios. Located at the center of the St. Petersburg Museum of Anthropology, it remains a popular attraction today.

CHAPTER ELEVEN

[1] Stanzas 6–8 of Nikolay Karamzin's "Spring Song of a Melancholic" (1788).

[2] A Russian Orthodox Church service comparable to a mass.

[3] Willow branches are part of the Russian Easter tradition and are on display in the city's main department store, Gostinyy Dvor, during that time of year.

[4] A type of shirt with the collar fastening at the side, popular among the proletariat between the two World Wars.